In Dreams

and other stories

Andrew Leggett

First published 2026 by
Ginninderra Press
PO Box 2 Bentleigh 3204
ginninderrapress.com.au

ACKNOWLEDGEMENTS

In Dreams has evolved from an earlier draft manuscript which was the creative component of my doctoral dissertation in Creative Writing at Griffith University: *In Dreams: A Novel and Its Exegesis, The Place of Dreams in the Novel and the Cinematic Work of David Lynch.* I offer my thanks to my supervisors Professor Nigel Krauth and Dr Anthony Lawrence for their support and assistance in the planning and development of that project. Thanks is also due to the members of my various writers' critique groups including Rosanna Licari, Dr Melissa Ashley, B.R. Dionysius, Dr Cheryl Hayden, Duncan Richardson, Sam Wagan Watson, Tamara Lazaroff, Michelle Taylor, Dr Jane Fenton Keane, Rob Morris and Joel Hopkinson, as well as to others who offered critical readings of drafts of Garrick Willis' poetry, the stories in this collection, or the manuscript of *In Dreams*, including Dr David Reiter, Dr Gershon Maller, Professor Bronwyn Lea, Dr Wendy Green, Ann Ralston and Linda Kaarina Holmberg.

The *In Dreams* chapter 'A night in the toolroom' evolved from a short story by the same name, published in *Social Alternatives*. The poems attributed to Garrick Willis first appeared in following publications: 'Wallaby Dreaming' in *The Weekend Australian Review of Books*, 'Broken for Me' in *Poetry Nottingham* (UK); 'The Idiot' in *Australian Family Physician* and 'Shadow' in *Stylus Poetry Journal*. Those first three poems were included in my first collection of poetry *Old Time Religion and Other Poems* (Interactive Press, 1998), as was Garrick's poem 'locket'. 'Shadow' appeared in my second collection *Dark Husk of*

Beauty (Interactive Press, 2006). Earlier drafts of that manuscript were highly commended for the Arts Queensland Thomas Shapcott Award and commended for IP Picks National Poetry Manuscript Award. Nick Myshkin's slam winning haiku won me the prize at the first Brisbane Writers' Fringe Festival, an event forged by Brett Dionysius and his committee, one that later became the Queensland Poetry Festival. 'Ratsak' first appeared in the literary journal *Heartland*. 'Kindness' was first published in *Text Journal of Writing and Writing Courses*. 'Chesed' first appeared in *Idiom 23*, 'Taxidermist' in *Social Alternatives*, 'Barry White' in *StylusLit*, 'Journey to Glasgow' in *e.ratio postmodern poetry journal* and 'Squid' in *Sudo Journal*.

CONTENTS

Part 1: In Dreams

Part 2: Other Stories

PART ONE
IN DREAMS

SOMETHING FUNNY HAPPENED

The Pacific Highway can be a real bastard when you're stuck between petrol tankers drag-racing. Garrick Willis parked his black BMW in the basement of the main building at the Princess Alexandra Hospital, walked to the Dutton Park Station, and took the train down to do his clinic at Logan Hospital. This gave him time to catch up on *JAMA* and the *New England Journal of Medicine*.

At lunch time, Garrick boarded the return train at Meadowbrook, taking the only vacant seat in the carriage, next to a tall skinny man in black jeans, a studded belt, white tee shirt and upturned-pointy-toed black boots. Garrick fixed his gaze on the man's dark coiffe, gelled to a horn in front, just like the Leningrad Cowboys. It fascinated him, as much as a lady's little hat might, should she pin it on, getting ready for the races. This fellow's earlobes were distended, with huge piercings rimmed with onyx rings. Stylised serpents ran down from his arm, through the bend of his right elbow and down the forearm, all the way to his slender wrist. Garrick noted track marks and moved his butt a little to the right, away from the stranger.

As his neighbour chomped away on nicotine gum, Garrick sat stiff on the edge of the bench and stared at a spot about 5cm inside the back of the head of woman occupying the seat in front of him. When she left the carriage at Kuraby station, Garrick reached down to open his briefcase, hesitated, and then decided against it. As the train moved on, with the traffic on Beenleigh Road flashing past the window at the stranger's left shoulder, strong as the urge might be, this was not the time to pull out the *New England Journal*. Not the thing to do up so close to someone, who, if he reads at all, struggles to get past the cover of *International Tattoo* or *Prick Magazine*.

With the rush of the train, sunlight flickered through the gaps between the palings of the fences that separated the rail line from suburban wilderness. Garrick noticed his travelling companion's right arm spasm. A few sharp jerks followed, of that arm only, and nothing else. Then the stranger slumped a little into the seat, his teeth clacking together as his jaws chomped. The man came around with a start, looked down at the small patch of damp in the crotch of his jeans, glanced quickly to his right, muttering 'Sorry, Jade, sorry!' None of the other passengers seemed to notice, but, to Garrick, the diagnosis was immediately evident.

It was not so much the complex partial seizure that troubled him, nor the stranger's ejaculation, but the name spoken in his postictal daze, the utterance of that particular name. It brought on a chill under Garrick's skin, crawling from one shoulder to the other. An unpleasant tingle ran down his spine, just like when his fifth-grade teacher screeched a fresh piece of chalk across the blackboard. It was as though the speech was harbinger of some horrific event yet to be suffered by the one who bore the name, a name on the edge of which Garrick teetered, losing his balance on the verge of the abyss of *amore*.

After the train slid to a halt at Dutton Park Station, Garrick grabbed his briefcase and strode off towards the barriers. He was not usually so determined to make his way across the Translational Research Institute campus towards Building 15, at the hub of the hospital designed to look like the Starship Enterprise warping its way through hyperspace.

Garrick wanted to put as much fresh air as possible between him and the man with the serpents, the seizures, and the stiff black coiffe.

The hair on the back of Garrick's neck was rising under his button-down collar, prompting him to look back over his shoulder. There, about twenty metres back, the coiffe was following, now with a grey canvas knapsack slung across one shoulder and a cigarette smouldering out of the left corner of his mouth. The stranger did not return his gaze. He didn't duck, nor did he wave. He showed no sign of pleasure or aversion. Garrick reached the tunnel beside the basement car park and kept walking until he reached Building 15. He caught the lift and pushed the button to the second floor. Through the gap before the lift doors closed, Garrick saw the stranger stubbing out his butt and chucking it into the waste bin as he entered the building.

On the second floor. Garrick nodded hello to the receptionist as he passed, dumping his briefcase beside the desk in Consulting Room 4. He registered disgust at the pile of bowls and cups in the hand basin. He drew the blue curtain around the sink and the clinical couch, pulled out his prescription pads and booted up the computer, hoping that none of his patients would require a serious examination.

Garrick stepped out into the reception area and picked up his first patient file and called for 'Nicholas Myshkin!' The man with the coiffe rose from his seat, picked up his grey rucksack and stepped towards Garrick, who extended his hand. 'I'm Dr Garrick Willis.'

'Call me Nick, Doc! Funny thing that was, you sitting next to me on the train. Do you get down Logan way often?'

'Yes, it was strange. I do a clinic at Logan Hospital, one morning a week. Come this way.' Garrick ushered his patient through with a sweep of his hand. 'Take a seat over there.'

Garrick arranged the furniture so that his swivel chair faced the computer. He'd set the patient's chair at a right angle to his desk, so the man would sit with his back to the curtain. Garrick turned around to ask Nick, 'So, how can I help you?'

'Haven't you read my doctor's letter?'

'I'm interested in hearing directly what's bothering you.'

'Whatever, let's just get on with it.'

The note from Christine Smythe at the Highgate Medical Centre went:

Dear Garrick,

Thank you for seeing Nick Myshkin, a 42 yo musician (on DSP for ADHD) with chronic pain. Nick sees me frequently for scripts: codeine, Valium, dexamphetamine. Today refused. Became aggressive, then suddenly blank staring. Noted eyes flicking to left before right hand banging on my desk. Lasted about ten seconds. Patient disorientated after. Muttered 'Sorry, Jade'. Then noticed where he was and asked 'what happened?' Epilepsy? Relevance to risk of violence? CT brain scan with and without contrast negative. Hep C +ve. HIV −ve. Needs EEG? Over to you to investigate, initiate therapy at your discretion.

Regards
Chris Smythe

'Are you aware of what Dr Smythe has written?'
'More or less. She said I was cranky when she wouldn't write me a

new script, then something funny happened. Seems like I scared her. I don't remember doing anything.'

'So what do you make of it?'

'I don't know. You're the specialist!'

'Has anything like this ever happened to you before?'

'Sometimes I lose track of time and end up somewhere. Don't know how I got there. Once I woke up in bed with a blonde girl in a trucker's motel. I remembered having a few drinks. She told me I'd been doing some strange stuff. But now she comes round and gives me a blow job whenever she wants some ice. Maybe she likes the scary stuff.'

'You do much ice?'

'A bit, now and then.'

'And other drugs?'

'I smoke a bit of weed. I like a drink. I'll do smack if I can get it. And speed. I like the ice, but it makes me cranky and people tell me I do weird shit when I'm on it.'

'Like?'

'Well, this chick says I was chasing her round, swinging a crowbar. That sort of shit.'

'What do you think of that?'

'Well, heavy shit, if it happens. Maybe it should worry me, but it doesn't, because I don't remember it.'

'Do you make the stuff, or just sell it?'

'Don't make it, although I sometimes pass some Pseudofed from Vietnam on to the guy that's got the lab. Don't deal much either. Just to the musos I play with, and a bit to the chicks that hang out with the band. Big time guy's got tight connection with the ones who run the clubs. Doesn't like me cutting in ... but what's it to you, anyway?'

'I'm going to ask you about some things that sometimes happen to people who have the kind of condition I think you might have ...'

'Okay!'

'And I want you to tell me if they ever happen to you.'

'Fire away.'

'Do you ever smell funny smells?'

'Yeah, Doc. Like when you farted?'

Garrick Willis considered himself to be a cut above most of his physician colleagues when it came to sensitivity and attunement. But this grinning deadbeat was definitely getting his goat. *This arsehole isn't worth it.* Garrick took a deep breath and carried on.

'No, weirder than that. Now look, I'll be straight with you. I think you're here today because you want help with something that you don't understand or know much about, but it frightens you. You have no idea how to let someone help you, so you act like a smartarse clown. But this isn't school. I am trying to understand this weird stuff that happens to you, so I can help you manage it, maybe even stop it from happening. Can we go on now?'

'If you've finished the lecture, Doc, I'll pull my head in! You do your stuff.'

'All right then. So tell me about the smells?

'Well sometimes when I'm banging a girl, it just comes on, like burning rubber.'

'Any other strange sensations come on with the funny smell?'

'Sometimes things look really big, then they shrink right down and are really little again.'

'Mmm. Anything else?'

'Sometimes I hear a noise like a train engine chuffing in my head. And I can get a weird queasy feeling that starts in my belly and crawls down my body into my legs. Objects seem to turn onto odd angles, and I see coloured lights. Then sometimes I lose it. Well, once that started in a nightclub, when the strobes came on. I lost it and didn't come around for twenty minutes or so. People said I was thrashing around on the floor. They called the ambulance. I thought I must've just had a bad pill.'

'Did they take you hospital?'

'No, the ambos wanted to, but I wouldn't let them. I had too much shit in my system. I just told them to fuck off, took a cab home and slept it off.'

'I see you're hepatitis C positive. It's easier to treat now? I could refer you to the clinic for it.'

'Doc, they wouldn't take me unless I'd gone to rehab first. And stayed clean for a while. I started on the program once, but dropped out after the first couple of shots. It was like having a permanent head cold.'

'Yes, interferon injections can do that. But there's a new drug that's not so bad, and treatment that doesn't take so long. We could talk more about that ...'

'Maybe later, Doc. Let's just deal with the weird stuff for now.'

'Are you still sharing needles?'

'No, Doc. Always use cleanskins now. Bit of a scare, that.'

'But you let girls go down on you without a condom?'

'You only live once, Doc! So what do you think it is?'

'Well, I'm almost certain that you suffer with epilepsy, and the strange sensations and movements, and maybe even the violent episodes you don't remember, are what we call complex partial seizures, caused by some focus of abnormal electrical activity somewhere in the brain. When you fell down and were thrashing on the floor in the night club, that was what we call a grand mal seizure, brought on by flashing strobe lights stimulating a wave of electrical activity that generalises throughout your whole brain and causes you to have a fit.'

'So why me?'

'It's more common than you think. About one in twenty-five people has some form of epilepsy.'

'Not in my family.'

'It's not usually hereditary.'

'Well, what the fuck did it then?'

'Most commonly it's due to some part of the brain being injured when you're a baby, not getting enough oxygen during the birth process. The brain has a little horn that sits inside the skull just behind your ears. That part is especially sensitive to lack of oxygen, and most easily damaged. Many of the symptoms you have could originate from an abnormal electrical focus there, due to scarring. Another cause of that can be the long fits that some little children have when you have a high temperature. Did your mother ever tell you anything like that?'

'I was taken away by Children's Services when I was three, Doc. They said she was an alky prostitute, not a fit mother. None of my foster parents knew anything about that kind of stuff.'

'Sorry to hear that. You've had a rough time, haven't you?'

'I just get on the best I can. So what do we do about this epilepsy shit?'

'Well, there's medication. But you don't start that until we've done some tests to make a definite diagnosis. And you must stop using amphetamines. They can kindle the abnormal electrical focus and make things much worse.'

'Fat chance! What tests, Doc?'

'Well, Dr Smythe has already done a CT brain scan, and that's negative, so it's not likely this is due to a tumour or a blood clot. Sometimes it can be. We should do an MRI scan, too, because there can be tumours, knots of small blood vessels, and other abnormalities in the brain that show up better on that kind of scan. And if you've been injecting ice, it can make small blood vessels in the brain to seize up and cause mini strokes that leave little holes in the white matter like those in Swiss cheese.'

'That's heavy, Doc!'

'Well, it is, but we have a three-month waiting list for MRI brain scans, when it's not an emergency. But in the meantime, we must do an EEG with photic stimulation.'

'What sort of shit is that?'

'An electroencephalograph—a test for which we put a little cap on your head and tape some electrodes to your skull.'

'You mean shock treatment?'

'No, there's no electricity going into the wires. They are there so we can measure the electrical activity coming out of the brain in the area under the part of your skull that the wire's taped onto. We don't give you any shock. That's a different machine.'

'Well, thank Christ for that!'

'We send flashing lights into your eyes during the test and watch the trace for a response.'

'Sounds like fun! I guess you'd better book me in.'

'Do you drive?'

'No, Doc, not since I came off my bike on the Gold Coast Motorway and cracked my head.'

'Well, sometimes a bang on the head can cause it, but there's nothing to show on the CT scan. It's possible that you could have a seizure while riding your bike. That could cause you to have an accident. So don't take up driving again now. And one more thing: Dr Smythe mentioned someone called Jade in her letter? Who is Jade?'

'She's the one that drops 'round for ice every now again. The one that gives me head jobs.'

Garrick showed Nick out. He asked the receptionist to book the tests, and the follow-up appointment.

BROKEN FOR ME

Garrick poured himself a glass of Traminer, picked up his Blu-ray remote from the coffee table, flicked on *Blue Velvet* and flipped forward to the scene where Ben, with the face paint, picks up a stage light and lip synchs Roy Orbison's *In Dreams*. Slumped on his couch, Garrick downed the wine with three spring rolls and a Vietnamese lemon grass braised beef rice vermicelli salad. The encounter with the new patient had left him quite unsettled. He couldn't stop ruminating on Nick's strange utterance, during the seizure—'Sorry, Jade, sorry!'

Garrick's concentration was shot. He'd gotten nowhere with analysis of the eye movements of the shoplifters he had lined up in the lab last Wednesday, wired to the electroencephalograph, watching *Clockwork Orange*. He was hoping to identify patterns, genetically determined, that might predict recidivism, contributing an evidence base for sentencing offenders. No longer would magistrates be left to rely on eugenics and phrenology. So far the only pattern he could discern from his observations was the disappearance, from his office, of several issues of *Ralph* magazine, a pale green flower vase and various items of stationery. These losses always followed *in vivo* laboratory sessions with volunteer subjects who'd responded to the notice he posted in the foyer of George Street Law Courts.

Garrick paused the disc just as Jeffrey Beaumont, bruised and battered, woke in the field where he was abandoned after Frank Booth took his pleasure at the end of that wild ride. Garrick was falling asleep. Time to call it a night.

So he was, at 10 p.m., sprawled across the bed in his Dornoch Terrace unit, staring at the print on the wall—a black-and-white photograph of a blonde woman, her hair blown back by the whoosh of the rollercoaster in some fun park in the 1930s, her eyes alight. One hand clutched the safety bar, the other struggled against the breeze that revealed the silk above her stockings pushing back against the hemline of her flounced skirt.

Garrick had fallen in love with this rollercoaster goddess. It seemed like he was plunging from heaven, headlong into a bottomless elevator shaft, leaving the contents of his stomach behind on several floors. Although Jade had long since left to work the late shift, Garrick was drawn like a lamb on a shepherd's crook into the fold of her absence. In a couple of hours, wouldn't she return?

Jade kept her cottage near the 'Gabba Cricket Ground, said it helped her to feel less claustrophobic. She slept there sometimes. He rested his head on her pillow, allowing him to lose himself, falling into it. When he lay where she had been, missing her, he wanted to smoke. He caught himself reaching for the gold foil of her near-empty packet on the bedside table.

Then he pulled his hand back, as the movement woke the memory of three cigarettes, after sharing the second litre bottle of Frascati, at Romeo's restaurant, on a rare long weekend in Airlie Beach late in the eighties, away from Bowen Hospital, in those optimistic days of the bullet-proof suit. That time, the nausea came on as he stumbled out the door after settling the bill. He staggered back to the hotel, repeatedly falling over Penny, who was then his wife, lay down on the bed as the room began to spin. He vomited *fettucini pescatore* all night.

Garrick withdrew from touching the gold foil and cellophane and reached instead for the page on which he'd printed a recently drafted poem. He picked it up and settled into pining for Jade, reading his own text over again until he drifted into sleep:

Broken For Me

Before she woke,
he turned to her and kissed
the cracked lips of the dawn,
taking from her mouth
the eucharist of dried saliva.
He knew nothing
of its transubstantiation
to a fleshy rose
that would stick in his throat,
take root in his chest
and press its thorns
deep into the base of its skull.
His only thoughts were of the beauty
of her fierce red acne
that blossomed in the first two months
of oral contraception
and the dull sense of relief
that it was her body
that was being broken.

*

Garrick was an onlooker in his own dream. He watched himself walking in a strange city, a much older city than Brisbane, more like the oldest parts of Hobart, or of old Sydney down by the Rocks. Darkness surrounded him. Darkness followed him. The gas lamps dimmed as he approached, then returned to incandescence when he'd passed. From a fourth storey window on the left-hand side of the street, a gravelly voice bawled out several verses of *Good Night, Irene*. The street was too narrow. He passed a row of squalid, sandstone Georgian terraces, his boots clomping across the cobblestones and splashing through a fetid puddle rising up from a blocked drain. Sacks of garbage lay strewn across the pavement, broken into by dogs. The air stank of rotting prawns and decaying vegetable matter, in spite of the chill. The rain drizzled down. Although the collar of his long black coat was turned up snug, gusts of wind stung his face with sleet. Overhead, a brown moon attempted to peek out through a thin patch in the cloud cover. In spite of the weather, the expression he observed on the face of dream-Garrick was one of resolute purpose.

He turned left into an alley between buildings constructed out of red convict brick. At the end of the lane there was a wall from which a single spotlight shone its beam onto an old MG convertible, reflecting from the bright red duco. On the driver's side, the black racing wheel and gear stick knob contrasted sharply with the cream kid leather of the seat. On the passenger side, a substantial form could be made out, covered in a white canvas sheet through which something crimson seeped.

Garrick watched his shadow-self approach the vehicle and lift the sheet from the passenger side, exposing the corpse of a blonde woman in a short black dress, her cherry lipstick smeared all over her cheeks and chin, her throat ripped open. His eyes rested on the tattoo on her left shoulder, torn into a shapeless symbol by the marks of savage teeth. A dozen men in black uniforms with peaked caps sprang out and surrounded shadow-Garrick, drawing Smith and Wesson .38s, menacing his head. Out of the shade of a rusty fire-escape stepped a sad-eyed Police Commissioner, gesturing an order to lower hardware.

The Commissioner stepped forward, bowed his head and clasped shadow-Garrick in a powerful handshake. As the Commissioner's grip tightened, his face morphed into that of Nick Myshkin, the patient he'd encountered on the train, whose strange utterances had unnerved him. Commissioner Myshkin gripped shadow-Garrick by the shoulders and leaned in close to whisper a secret greeting in the condemned man's left ear.

Watching Garrick strained to read the Commissioner's lips. He thought he made out the words *I am Judas, and with this kiss, I seal the repetition of events*, but the sound was muffled.

Then he noticed a cherry-red stain on shadow-Garrick's cheek. The Commissioner turned away, shook his head, and offered a thumbs down signal to his men. Garrick watched as his was forcibly cuffed and escorted up the lane towards the dog-box of a black paddy wagon. He screamed against his closed glottis, then screamed and screamed again until, from somewhere far away and long ago, the sound of screaming came.

*

Garrick's scream was interrupted by Jade elbowing him in the chest. She turned to him and looked into his face with her wide green eyes.

A lipstick smear from a hot pink kiss rode lewd against the shadow of his salt-and-pepper stubbled cheeks. 'That must've been some dream, honey! You've been squeezing me so tight I couldn't breathe. I need a cuddle.' She giggled. 'Come and give me a kiss.'

'When did you come in?'

'Just a few minutes ago. When I lay down here beside you, you were thrashing about and kicking. I thought you must be having a nightmare.'

'No, I couldn't've been. You can't thrash about when you're dreaming. In dreaming sleep, your muscles are completely paralysed.'

'Thanks for the lecture. So why am I imagining that you're kicking me?'

'Well, was I snoring?'

'Sometimes you do, but not this time. Why do you ask that?'

'Well, if I had sleep apnoea, I'd snore when I was obstructing. I'd thrash about and kick my legs when I stopped breathing.'

'And what am I supposed to do then?'

'The thrashing and kicking would jolt me out of it, get me going, make me breathe again.'

'And what if it didn't?'

'You're a nurse. Resuscitate me.'

'Yeah, I could give you the kiss of life.'

'That would be fun.'

Jade tossed her head and pouted her lips at him. 'Well, were you dreaming? You were kicking me, and my legs are covered in bruises!'

She did bruise, only too easily. Such a fragile thing, really. And so often gone, like a genie, in a puff of smoke. Returning to his bidding, whenever he wished for her, whenever he took hold of the lamp and gave it a little rub.

'Did I bump you?.'

'Bump me? Look at this one then. She drew her pale left calf from under the sheets and pointed to the purple patch.

'Gee! Sorry, Jade.'

'So you are dreaming and kicking. How does Professor Willis explain that?'

'Well, maybe the dream isn't happening in REM sleep, like most dreams do, but in deeper stage IV sleep, the stage in which sleep walking and sleep talking happens. Do I ever talk in my sleep?'

'Not much, not that I've noticed.'

'But sometimes I do?'

'Yeah, sometimes.'

'What do I say?'

'Not much. Sometimes you mutter. Sometimes I hear you say things like "Sorry, Jade!" I wonder then what kind of bad boy you've been, what you might've been up to when I'm gone.' She grinned wickedly, then her smile disappeared when she noticed that he didn't seem to find that funny. 'So tell me about the dream.'

'I wouldn't want to trouble you.'

'You know, when I woke you, you looked like a little frightened boy, visited by the bogeyman.'

'Well, maybe I've had something like night terrors. I used to have them when I was a kid. Dad said that I would run around the house with my eyes wide open, pointing at something in the air, screaming. He would grab me and shake me awake. When I did, I would tell him that I'd had a bad dream, but I couldn't remember it.'

'Well, can you remember this one?'

'No, not really, I can't now.'

'I think you remember some that you're not telling me,' she sulked.

'Well, maybe, but it's like when I was a kid. The scary dream fragments would slip away from me and defy translation into stories. I couldn't talk about them coherently. Like dreams in movies. But only sometimes. Some movie dreams are stories, but the dreams in films aren't really dreams, are they?'

'Then what are they?'

'Well, there's this thing called the oneiric metaphor, but maybe it's not really a metaphor, but an endless series of hints, of hidden messages, a trail of anamorphoses ...'

Jade's eyes rolled back in her head as she raised her eyebrows. Just before her mouth closed over his, he caught the scent of lime vodka cruisers on her breathe. He glanced up at the clock on the wall. It was 1.30 a.m.

'Just shut up and fuck me,' she said.

*

Jade was determined to make Garrick notice she was different to his ex-wife, Penny. She put on blue eye shadow, black mascara, bright red lipstick and a generous spray of that French perfume he'd given her on Valentine's Day. She strapped on her cork wedge sandals, pulled on a tight white t-shirt, stepped into her green suede miniskirt and cocked her pelvis provocatively, fluttering her lashes as she looked back at him over her shoulder and called for him to zip her up.

Jade giggled. Garrick dealt with the zipper and the hook, then wrapped his hairy arms tight around her waist, pushing up under her t-shirt. 'You're a naughty boy,' she said. 'We'll never get to Espressohead if you start that!'

On the way Boundary Street, Garrick told her, 'Tom's sleeping over again tonight.'

'He'll be swinging on the cupboard doors again,' Jade said. 'I wonder what he'll smash this time?'

'Don't be like that! He loves cuddling up to you!'

'No wonder! You leave it to me to change his sheets when he wets the bed.'

'Well, he likes you. And he knows you are good to him.'

'He misses his mother. She's always pushing him on to you when I'm around. I think she does it too much for a little one his age. Sometimes when you duck out I have to put up with him screaming for her. I just can't console him. He knows he's not mine and I can't compete with her. I wonder if we'll ever have one of our own?'

Garrick screwed up his face and said, 'It's a bit early for us to be thinking about a baby, isn't it? I'm not even divorced, yet!'

'No matter what I do to try to please you, and bring you out of your misery, I don't think you'll ever want to marry me.'

'It's just too soon for us to be talking about that.'

'Well at least you could get a divorce.'

'I'm working on it. I've been to see a lawyer, and she's started negotiations. Let's just forget about all that for now and try to have a good day.'

Jade pouted. *If that's all I get for speaking my mind, maybe I should go out. Say I've picked up an agency shift ...*

They were on Boundary Street now, and Garrick picked up pace as they approached Espressohead.

Jade chuntered on to herself. *There he goes, striding off in front of me like a marathon runner, just to claim his favourite table. When I catch up with him, he'll be off as soon as I sit down, up to the newsagent to buy his newspaper, plump himself down in front of me, open it like a shield against me and bury himself in it. I hope he doesn't race off to the cake shop up the road and bring back a box full instead of getting stuff that's on the menu. I'd better order a long black ...*

*

Garrick settled himself into his chair at the table at which he sat every Saturday morning. He opened the *Weekend Australian* to the books section. He began to sip his extra-shot *latte*, wrapping the glass in a paper napkin. Reaching for the Paris breast from the French patisserie, he noticed that he was not sharing it with Penny, but with some fiercely sexual creature with spiky blonde hair and lots of pale freckled thigh showing below the hem of that ridiculous skirt. He reached across under the table and stroked the fine down, causing her to jerk away and arch her spine to the frissons of current generated from their sacral origin. *Here I am, with my girl, and shit! I can't stop ruminating like a neurologist, or as if I'm directing a movie, and she's just one of the characters shot by the camera.*

Jade seemed twitchier today, drumming her fingers compulsively, making sideways glances at the barista, who was struggling to clean congealed milk froth off the steam spout of the espresso machine.

Then Garrick saw it, on page three of the *Review of Books*—his poem—the one he'd written when he was beginning to recognise the chasm opening between him and Penny. Jumping out at Jade from behind the wall of paper, he startled her. 'It's here!' He thrust the paper at her, pointing at the column of text at the bottom of the page.

When she made out his name in bold type, she squealed, 'Wow, Garrick! You're in the paper—such a clever weasel.'

Then Jade insisted that he read it to her aloud:

Wallaby Dreaming

There is an old killing in the place
and he is drawn up the gully rock hopping.
The afternoon is failing as he jumps
between the trunks of fallen eucalypts
and limestone outcrops. Cicadas
and the gum flowers fill the air
with scent and roaring. He stumbles
at a landfall, missing the ledge.
Both knees are grazed. Below
the wallaby people are making their dreaming
in the clearing on the high kikuya.
The light is failing and the dew is settling
on the skin of the intruder. Somehow
he is spared.

Later that evening, she is driving.
He is drawn too late to warning
as the wallaby blind to the high beam lights
jumps at the bumper of the green Charade.

The warclub thuds, the car
skidding across the road before braking.
The air is full of animal rubber fear.
She and the beast are whimpering.
The wallaby has smashed a femur.
He takes the wheel and ploughs
the front wheel drive from first to reverse
from reverse to first again
across the neck he loves.
He is killing his dreaming.

'Oh Garrick! I'm so pleased for you.'

TOO LITTLE, TOO LATE

After Garrick read little Tom to sleep, he and Jade spent an irritable Saturday evening in bed. Both quickly lost interest in the rugby league match on television. 'Why do we have to watch this boring crap?' he snapped when the Broncos were down 22-0 to the Melbourne at half time.

'I thought you supported the Broncos!' said Jade. 'You're impossible to please. I can never get it right! Now you want to make me feel stupid again.'

'I hate seeing them balls it all up. It's pathetic. Big men running around in shorts and fluorescent boots tumbling each other into the turf and busting cruciate ligaments.'

'I don't like seeing my team go down so badly either.'

'No, I think you're just reminiscing about the time that forward picked you up when you were back in college, doing athletics training, at ANZ Stadium. Back when they used to train there too. Wasn't he a bit rough with you?'

Jade's face wrinkled and stiffened. Garrick felt her limbs go rigid. She turned her back on him and curled like a foetus, tucking her knees under her chin. Garrick leaned on his elbow and looked her over. A tear was forming in the corner of her exposed left eye, ready to run down her cheek. She always did this when she was getting ready for a good cry.

Garrick got up and turned off the television. He returned to bed, reached for Jade with both arms and forced her to face him. He closed his mouth on hers and held her as she sobbed and beat his chest with her fists. Her nipples stood up like cherries on gelatine desserts, made to be bitten. He moved his mouth to nibble at her left ear lobe. Jade tensed her neck like a turtle and began to giggle. Garrick stiffened. He nuzzled her ear and whispered, 'I'm sorry. I couldn't give a shit about the Broncos, win or lose.'

She giggled, sprang around and said, 'Tell me about what it would be like with Rachel!'

She must breathe through her nose, he thought, kneading her breasts and telling her about things he wished he'd done with her Canadian friend, the girl who sometimes sun-baked topless on his balcony with Jade on Saturdays.

At first few minutes, Garrick relaxed, but then his anxiety mounted with the awareness of losing control. He fought the intrusive images, but they came regardless, disrupting his sense of blissful merger, as he saw himself ripping Jade open with a kitchen knife. He pushed her away, roughly. She looked up at him, offended. 'What did you do that for?'

'Sorry, honey,' he said. 'It was just too much for me.'

'Too much of a good thing, I suppose?'

'It was so good. Then suddenly I began to feel terrified of losing you.' The images had gone now. There was no need for her to know.

Jade glanced at the bedside alarm clock, showing 9:45 p.m. She kissed Garrick and rose, telling him, 'I've just got time to shower, get into my uniform and get to work.'

'I thought you weren't due to start night shift again for another three weeks.'

'They rang while I was out at the video store. Someone's called in sick, so they offered me an extra shift.'

Garrick groaned. Jade's nakedness faded like a ghost at the bathroom door.

Jade showered, then returned to dress. She exited the bathroom a little after 10.00 p.m. Garrick noticed the opacity of her navy uniform. The shapeless knee-length front-buttoning garment left him wondering which hospital's staff had contributed the naughty nurse fetish to popular culture. Back in his student days, at least the nurse's uniforms had been white and transparent enough to enable a fair guess. The way some wore them, there was little room for guesswork. Watching Jade from behind, he was reminded that he should be grateful that work was the only place that she wore flat shoes and conservative underwear. He yelled out, 'You should take up that hem about six inches if you want to pick up anyone tonight.'

She turned around to him, pretended to frown, and shook her finger. 'You're a very bad boy!' She blew a kiss to him and disappeared, leaving him lying with all that space beside him in bed.

When Garrick found out which hospital it was that insisted their nurses dress in strict accordance with the fetish, he would apply for a position there as Executive Director of Medical Services. It certainly wasn't the Princess.

In spite of the ceiling fan continuously whopping the air like a helicopter rotor, the bedroom remained oppressively humid. Garrick tossed about and kicked off the sheets. There was something quite strange about Jade's new enthusiasm for overtime.

Sleep now seemed impossible without her. After sex, a cloud of tenderness seemed to envelope them, like unborn twins sharing a single amniotic sac. When she curled up against him, her body fitted so neatly into the nest his made, as he wrapped himself around her from behind. This was the way they lay together, each on their left side, his right arm wrapped around her waist, with his hand resting her belly.

Garrick could not rest in the emptiness between his sheets that night. When the storm broke about 1.00 a.m., he found relief in the crashing thunder, the flashes of luminosity at the window and the beating of rain against the glass.

*

In the dream, no matter how Garrick tried to run, he found himself moving slowly, like a 16 mm film reel, wound by hand from one frame to another, moving at the speed of terror, always too little, too late. His feet were lead weights, and his passage through the air was like that of a wooden spoon through molasses. Somehow he made it up past the Laundromat on the corner of Harcourt and Brunswick Streets, crossed the road, jumped the gate and through the main entrance. He charged down the poorly lit corridor of the old boarding house. A termite-infested staircase with a broken bannister and a rift in the middle led to the upper level on the left, just inside the entrance. Old paisley paper curled and lifted from the walls, revealing cracked plaster and the stain of paste eaten by skittering American cockroaches. A smell kicked up at him from the decomposing carpet, like that of mould mixed with stale vodka and industrial cleaning products, the stench of nameless dread.

This woke up memories of his grandfather's grave dug nine feet down, deep into the clay of the Lismore cemetery, to make room for Grandma, who'd be joining him later. Six feet down, a green line marked the seepage into the soil of body fluids from the 108-year-old neighbour's coffin.

Liquid doom rushed through his veins as he came to the flaking timber door of number 6. From somewhere, he could hear his animal scream as he ran the door with his shoulder, rebounded, then picked himself up and threw himself at the slab again and again, until the hinges began to give. With another thrust, the screws wrenched free of their moorings, giving a scream of their own as they ripped their way out of the wood. He fell inwards with the door, bouncing off it as it landed, thudding like a terrible drum. The smell that punched his nostrils was acetone, sweet almonds, urine and a salty tang of blood.

On the far side of the bed, a tall thin man, with an extravagantly gelled coiffe, lay snoring, face into the pillow, his right arm hanging down beside the bed, the hand still encased in a bloodied garden glove, wrapped around the neck of a litre bottle of Stolichnaya, more than half gone.

The axe lay on the floor beside him, skewed to the right of the bed at a forty-degree angle, the blade facing outwards, sullied by the soft white matter, strands of hair and other tissues, congealed and clotted. It brought to mind a specimen that Garrick, as a medical student, had seen in a jar at the pathology museum—a tumour of the womb in which the structure of the tissues had become so chaotic that the core of it had come to hold a fluid cyst lined with skin, out of which grew long strands of hair sparsely scattered between outcrops of great jagged teeth.

What was left of Jade lay wrapped in a torn batik-patterned kimono in the middle of the bed, her face cloven through the right cheek, her teeth in similar disarray to those of the tumour in the pathology pot. The gash extended through to the socket of her right eye, which protruded—vitreous humour seeping through the rupture. The robe hung open, showing the wounds. The spikes of broken ribs protruded through her left breast, from which the blackened blood continued to extravasate and pool in the recess of her umbilicus. Further down, it made a mat of sticky silk in the little vee she'd trimmed above her bruised and swollen lips.

As Garrick screamed, the delicate membranes that separated the compartments of his mind ruptured, and the separate fractional essences of his being ran together all at once. He staggered to the bed, lay down beside the corpse, and wrapped himself around her. In doing so, he paused his screaming for long enough for some mute, black, bat-winged thing to burst out from his throat and fly away with the force of the first of a multitude of sobs.

THE ANGEL MORONI

Nick stepped out through the doors of the Kentucky Fried Chicken franchise on Main Street, Woolloongabba, his belly full of Coke, fries and fat. Nick was ready to face the night, whatever truckers it might bring across his way. He had several foil-wrapped refresher towels. There were no coasters to steal at KFC. *No gig tonight with the band. On again late at the Zoo next Saturday.*

The waning moon illuminated the golden statue of the Angel Moroni, standing on a granite plinth, trumpet raised, on the roof of the Mormon Temple. From this position of vantage, the Angel faced the place where the sun would rise tomorrow. Moroni watched over the houses between Main Street and Riverside Terrace, beyond six lanes of traffic, on the other side of the road.

Previous sightings of the statue inspired Nick to surf the net for information. He learned that the Latter Day Saints believe that Moroni, son of Mormon, was an ancient American warrior, the last of his Nephite tribe, to whom Jesus appeared and revealed essential teachings. This gospel was inscribed on golden plates, which Moroni buried before he died. Somehow resurrected as an angel, Moroni stood guard over the plates for many centuries before guiding the Prophet Joseph Smith to their secret location in 1838.

Nick also found that the website http//:theangelmoroni.com advertises steel-cut Angel Moroni ornaments at $9.99, packaged in an open-faced gold box, containing not only the crafted ornament, but also a printed lesson to assist the family in their endeavours to place

Christ back, where he belongs, in Christmas. It crossed Nick's mind that over the next two hours, the moon would set. By what light would the Angel see then, to watch over the temple, the city, the people, in the hours before dawn?

It's not so easy, life as an angel. So many to watch over, so many voices, so many prayers, so many scenes, so many places to be at once. Too much beauty. Too much pain. Too much information. Never to touch, never to intervene. Omniscience, with impotence. Weary as I am, I never rest.

Nick crossed Toohey Street and continued on. He reached Bromley Street just as he caught sight of her. There she was, in her high black boots and red tartan miniskirt, just over the street, leaning against the wall, on the right-hand side of the entrance drive of the Southern Cross Motel. Jittery, she moved her weight back and forth from one leg to the other, picked and fiddled with her skirt, clenched and unclenched her hands. Her straight jet-black hair, extending half way down her back, was stark in contrast with her pearlescent, slightly freckled skin. Eyes straining, he could just make out her nipples standing erect through the spandex of the white sports bra that was all she wore above the hips. She was hungry for it.

Nick watched a Volvo truck slow up, indicate and take the left turn into the motel drive. The driver signalled to the girl, and she followed. Nick watched her butt, and the rear end of the truck as it receded. *You are passing another Fox.*

Nick walked on to cross Baines Street at the lights, from the Thai restaurant on one side, to the Pineapple Hotel on the other. He bothered to wait for the walk signal, mindful of the news report of a teenager killed here, just the other week. He pushed the button when he reached the other side, repeating the ritual of the wait for the lights to change again before he could cross Main Street. He wandered up to the Night Owl, placed his backpack at this feet, leaned himself up against the wall next to the entrance, lit a cigarette, and waited for the call.

*

Nick trod the terracotta tiles past the reception and down the corridor to the lift, took the lift up to the first floor, turned right and walked the full length of the beige carpet to the door of room 27. He rapped three times in quick succession. The girl came to the door. Nick liked the way that skirt hung low over her bony hips.

She was agitated. The dragonfly hanging from her belly button stud quivered. Her long black hair swished when she turned and walked towards the trucker again.

He sat in the red armchair beside the bed, his huge hairy belly hanging over his boxers.

Nick caught a glimpse of her arse cheeks with the swing of her hips. *Now you see it. Now you don't. Here today, gone tomorrow.*

The girl sat herself down on the trucker's lap. Let him wrap those hams of arms around her, with their barbed wire tatts. Her arse began to gyrate on something that might have been the trucker's wiener, supposing he had one hidden away there, under all those rolls of fat.

'You wanna point?' said Nick.

The trucker nodded, nuzzling his bristly triple chin against the girl's fair neck, as she arched her back and began her theatrical repertoire of low soft moans. 'How much?'

'Sixty for the point, and another sixty for the girl's. And you pay 130 for the room. Another fifty for thirty minutes with the girl.'

'Anal?'

'An extra fifty for that.'

'Show me the gear ...'

'When you show me 350 smackeroos.' Nick took his right hand to loosen the strap and shrugged off the pack.

The trucker reached for his wallet on the bedside table and shelled out seven fifty dollar notes. Holding them in his right hand, he waved them to summon him over.

Nick took the notes and stuffed them into the hip pocket of his black Levi 511s. He reached into the pack, and pulled out a plastic zip-lock bag, full of smaller sealed transparent packages. He took a seat up at the pillow end of the bed beside the trucker's armchair and shook a couple of them out onto the red bedspread. He held one up for inspection. 'The crystal.'

'No Ratsak, battery acid? No shit like that?'

'100 per cent pure.'

'Then fix me up.'

Nick dipped into the backpack again and pulled out a sealed injection kit, a stainless steel soup spoon with the handle bent to ninety degrees at the spoon end, and a long black shoe lace. He tore the outer plastic open to unload five 1 ml syringes; five 29-gauge needles; three cotton filters; five alcohol wipes; and a couple of 5 ml plastic phials of sterile water. He took two syringes out of their packs, locked capped needles on, ripped the crystal packs open poured the contents into the spoon. Holding the spoon steady in his left hand, he uncapped a phial of sterile water with his right. He jiggled the spoon until the crystals dissolved, then popped a cotton filter into the solution. He placed the spoon, with the filter in its bowl, on the bedside table, picked up the first set, uncapped the needle, poked it into the cotton wad and drew the plunger. He turned the loaded syringe upside down and pushed, to expel the air bubble, then recapped and laid the fit down beside the spoon. He repeated this procedure with the second syringe, then picked up the cotton wad between his fingers, stuck it in his mouth, ground on it with his molars and sucked his cheeks in.

The trucker raised his eyebrows. Nick's glare told him he'd better not open his mouth.

Nick tied the shoelace round the trucker's left biceps, just below the extremity of the ink work. 'Make a fist. Clench and unclench.' Nick took the trucker's left paw, with its scratched 9 carat gold wedding band, in his own left and patted the back of it with his right, hoping to bring up a vein. *So much fat!* Just the same, that one looked a chance. 'Clench your fist again. Now let it go. And again.' Nick took the trucker's hand and patted the vein again. *Yes, this one should be a goer.* He tore open an alcohol wipe and swabbed the skin. *Just like cleaning the grease off my fingers after KFC.* Nick picked up the syringe, uncapped it. 'Put your hand out on the table there. Don't bump anything.' He held the hand still with his left, and slid the needle in with his right, secured it in place with the thumb and forefinger of his left, then drew back on the plunger. Blood shot back into the syringe. He gestured to the trucker to undo the shoelace, then pushed the meth into the vein.

'Jesus!' The trucker tensed, then sighed.

Now it was the girl's turn. She used to be easy, but now her veins were buggered up.

When it was done, Nick stuffed the rest into his pack, zipped it up, turned his back on them, walked to the door, let it close behind him and took the lift to reception, where he insisted on paying cash for the couple in room 27. The man at the desk must have been about that age. No questions asked. As for the night's takes, the rest would be the girl's.

*

Out on the street again, Nick lit another cigarette. Then he walked on, taking in the scene over the road. There had been an AFL game at the Gabba stadium earlier that evening. The Brisbane Lions had been done over in the home game by Collingwood, by a goal and two behinds. Some of the fans still hung around the Piney, wearing Lions guernseys, jackets and maroon and gold supporters scarves. The crew for the band that had been playing earlier on were packing the drum kit into the back of a Holden Rodeo utility truck. On Nick's side of the street, he came across a couple of likely looking boys outside the Night Owl, but he figured, from the way that they were eyeing each other up, they were more into it for fun than to earn what it took to keep them in tabs. He gave them a nod as he passed, and walked on towards the Story Bridge, to cross the span to hawk his wares to cougars in the Valley clubs. The golden Angel, with his trumpet raised, proclaiming the Restoration, stuck to his post.

GRAN'S DOCTOR

At around ten minutes past ten, Jade parked her Toyota Echo in the narrow carport of her cottage on Toohey Street, Kangaroo Point. Jade lived here with her grandmother until the old lady went into the nursing home at Annerley. As much as Jade hated that place, with its bins of soiled linen in the corridors and the smell of atomised meals coming from the kitchen, she would pay a brief visit tomorrow. Gran would not come home again. After a series of strokes, Gran could no longer feed herself. She would not see another Christmas.

The house would pass to Jade, now that her father was gone. He was Gran's only child, and she, in turn, his. She held Gran's power of attorney, enabling her to draw funds to pay the rates and other bills. She kept Gran's room untouched. A few of the old lady's nightgowns still were hanging in the dark-stained Tasmanian Oak closet. The wedding photo gathering dust on the bedside dresser showed Pop looking gaunt and severe in military uniform. They married in 1946, a fortnight after he returned from the prisoner-of-war camp in Burma. Gran and Pop had lived in this house while he worked as a technician at the Woolloongabba Telephone Exchange and finally, before retirement, in that great ugly Telstra tower. He didn't love the tower, but Pop had lived to work. He dropped dead, just two weeks after he retired, with a massive heart attack.

Gran had been admitted to the Princess when Garrick was on intake for neurology. His team arrived for their afternoon ward round while Jade was visiting, in uniform, about to leave to go to handover for the evening shift on the intensive care unit. He'd asked her to stay, not knowing she was family. He spoke so kindly to the old lady, and was so careful in the way that he examined her. He took time to demonstrate the signs to the students, without making Gran feel that she was a freak show. Jade was impressed. He seemed to be looking at her when he was talking to the students, giving orders to the registrar. Then he picked up Gran's hand carefully, and made eye contact. Jade had seen him before in the hospital canteen, and remembered the smart stitching on his suit, but had no idea who he was. She perked up when he asked her about Gran's blood pressure. She blushed and said, 'You'll have to ask a nurse. She's my grandmother.'

He seemed quite flustered, apologised profusely.

She took the opportunity to say: 'Actually, Dr Willis, I have a few things I would like to ask you about her condition. Do you mind if I call you when it's quiet a little later this afternoon?'

'Of course, I'd be glad to talk with you.' He turned to Gran. 'With your permission, of course, Mrs Carson?' asked Garrick, turning to address Gran.

Gran nodded and smiled the half smile she could just manage with the right side of her face sagging.

So it started. When Jade called Garrick on her dinner break, he was still in the hospital. He invited her around to the Specialist Neurologist's office. They spoke for half an hour. She was late back to ICU, his number punched into her phone contacts list.

A few days later, she asked if she could share his table in the staff dining room. And a week or so after that, he didn't seem surprised when she rang to ask him to take her to the nurses' ball. After the ball, they shared a bed, he whispered in her ear that she must never tell his colleagues how they met.

Jade crossed the verandah and turned the iron key in the lock. The door swung open. She reached inside to flick the light switch. The hallway stretched past Gran's room on the right and hers on the left, extending to the lounge with the open fireplace and high pressed metal ceilings, with another doorway through to the kitchen and the dining area. The floorboards were nine-inch polished pine—one of the first cottages in the area.

Jade opened the door to her room. This had been her father's room, when he was a boy. The silky oak bed with its steel-ringed tester, designed to hang mosquito nets, had not been his. It was something she had picked up at auction, stained as it was with dark pitch that a bored child had scratched all over with a nail or compass point, revealing for her the beauty of the grain, the potential reward for effort in restoration. It too many hours to strip it down, sand it back, and seal it. She transformed it into an object of beauty, beauty that would endure even when she, like the bed, had grown old, as her father had not.

Dad's suicide had featured on the front page of the Courier Mail. Mum was inconsolable. At the funeral, the recreational mourners at Our Lady of Mt Carmel formed a cordon of crows around her, while the little girl was left staring blankly at the mahogany box in the back of the hearse. After that, Mum's cancer progressed rapidly.

Not good now, to let Dad back into my mind. Too many reasons not to be alone here with so much waking up the memories.

Gran moved in then. *She nursed Mum right up until the end. And Mum passed away at home, the day before my eleventh birthday.* After the funeral, Gran organised the sale of the house, with packing and disposal of the contents. Jade's Mum left her everything she had, with Gran as trustee. At the end of that year, Gran took her out of Norman Park School and sent her to East Brisbane for Year 7. *It was strange going there, after what had happened to Dad. Mrs Doherty was extra nice to me, but I often heard the other teachers whispering about Dad when they passed me in the playground. It felt weird, like they had me packed in cotton wool. I was glad when that year was over.*

Jade's selection for the State Schools cross-country running team brought her a place among the cool kids in the eighth grade at Brisbane State High. It was good to move on there, to somewhere she could be herself and not the dead man's daughter.

At home, she continued to live under his shadow, in this room. She picked up her mobile phone, sent a quick text message to Rachel, unzipped her uniform and let it fall around her ankles. She stared for a while at her reflection, in the mirrored door of the old wardrobe, then opened the cupboard and pulled out a short black-and-white patterned stretch mini dress with a plunging back. She matched it with her meanest pair of red patent leather stilettos. She fixed her eyeliner and thickened her lashes with mascara.

*

Jade opened the door to greet Rachel Flanaghan as she pulled in outside the cottage and stepped out of the bucket seat of her beige VW Beetle. Rachel's short red velvet kimono rode up in that moment just after the car door opened. She wore a black choker with a white cameo and Barton black square-toed pumps with bows and Louis heels. Her long black hair swished and her hips swayed as she made her way up the steps. Most of the cat inked from her shoulder down her arm, all but the head, showed below the cuff of the sleeveless dress. 'Hello, Tiger!' said Jade, reaching out to plant a kiss on Rachel's cherry glossed lips.

'Well, hello to you too, Blondie! I'm the tiger all right, but by the look of you, I'd say we're cougars tonight!'

'Let's get into the Valley then and hit the dance floor.'

'Hell, girl, those boys will be so blown they'll lose control.' Rachel's Toronto accent made her seem even more exotic than her Eurasian features, with the woody scent of Opium on her freckled alabaster Irish skin. 'Where's Garrick tonight?'

'He's back at the unit with Tom. He thinks I've gone off to work at the Princess to do night shift. What an idiot!'

'You minx!' Rachel collapsed into Jade's arms laughing, nearly stumbling down the stairs on the way back out to the car. Rachel drove towards the Story Bridge, high above the coils of the broad brown snake of the Brisbane River, then across into Fortitude Valley. She spotted a street park on the left just across Brunswick Street. The girls walked the block back to The Family nightclub arm-in-arm, passed the scrutiny of the bouncer and the door bitch, and were soon inside leaning across the bar, sipping lime vodka cruisers and checking out the scenery as DJ Fluffy laid down her mix of the latest groove.

A couple of Indian girls in their early twenties were bollywooding. They drew male attention. A trio of pimply-faced Uni boys hovered, moonwalking awkwardly in their vicinity. All this, in spite of Fluffy playing Ricki-Lee!

Over in a corner, Jade spied a man closer to thirty, his long black coiffe protruding like a horn from behind a supporting pillar, together with the front end of his pointy-toed black suede boots. Jade downed the last of her second cruiser, grabbed Rachel by the arm and waltzed round the corner, parading in front of him. Just enough to catch his eye, then she sashayed onto the dance floor. He took the hint, took to his feet, and soon they found him bobbing up and down between them. 'Nick!' he said.

'Jade!'

'Rachel!'

They bobbed and wiggled their way through *Do It Like That*. In the brief lull in volume that signalled Fluffy's segue into the next mix, Nick placed an arm on each of the girl's shoulders and leaned in towards their ears. 'Would you ladies like a taste of something?'

The girls giggled and nodded, obediently following. Atomic Kitten came up with their cover of Blondie's *Heart of Glass*. Nick reached behind the pillar and pulled out a little backpack. He unzipped a pocket and took out a zip-locked plastic bag. 'Thirty dollars a tab, girls.' After handing over the cash, they each took an eccy and swallowed, then returned with Nick to the dance floor, just a little away from the leggy Lakshmi, curvy Saraswati and their ashram of devotees. The night was just beginning to liven up.

Nick drifted off for a while. They returned to the bar, watching Nick smooth his way into a number of other business transactions. By now they were laughing out loud and falling over each other. Rachel put her arm around Jade's shoulder and rested her hand on Jade's left breast. Jade felt her spine tingle. She steadied herself on her bar stool and ran her hand down Rachel's thigh.

Both girls were a little surprised when, around 2.00 a.m., Nick returned to them, leaned in, looked in turn into Rachel's dark almond eyes and Jade's round green ones, and said, 'I'd have something even more interesting to show you, ladies, if I was offered a bed for the night!'

A few minutes later, they were a trio of mutual chemical benevolence, a Jake-the-Peg, with Nick the extra leg between the two girls, one arm around the waist of each, heading down McLachlan Street towards the Beetle.

*

Back at Toohey Street, Jade put on a Rolling Stones CD. Nick soon had talked both girls round to trying crystal meth. 'Once you've taken it into the vein, you know you'll never go back to tabs or snorting shit like that,' he warned. Out came the packets, and the ninety degree spoon, as well as a fresh injection set. First Jade and then Rachel. Nick saved most of the point for himself. As the rush came on, they all danced a wild burlesque together, heading towards the bedroom, backed by Jagger singing *Satisfaction*. They partied in every imaginable way, until the girls collapsed into sleep. Just before dawn, Nick grabbed his backpack and slipped away, leaving two complimentary double passes to next Saturday's gig on the dresser, with his mobile number written on the back of each.

THE IDIOT

Garrick woke to the buzzer of the digital alarm clock drilling into his mind. His arm shot out to hit the snooze button, authorising the mechanism to repeat after five minutes.

Responding to the second assault, Garrick successfully located the off switch. He had slept badly. Reaching out for Jade, he found the space beside him empty. That space had been there now two mornings in a row. She had not returned since Saturday night, nor had she called or texted him. He missed her being there to kiss, but did not miss being told that his breath stank.

Garrick dragged himself out of bed, staggered to the bathroom, inhaled Nasonex, gargled Listerine. In the shower cubicle, he lathered his face from an aerosol can and shaved blind. He improvised a misanthropic blues when he nicked himself under his right ear, in exactly the same spot as the previous day.

> *I got out of bed*
> *When I was dead.*
> *I shaved my corpse*
> *And I kicked the cat ...*

For an hour or so after waking, Garrick was afflicted with a stream of drivel in the place of thought. It was as much as he could do to prevent himself from singing it aloud. Sometimes it was only the want of an audience that stopped him. In Jade's presence, there were times when that impulse came to be more than he could resist.

Garrick stepped out of the shower, dried himself on Jade's towel and pulled on his charcoal grey Elle Macpherson underpants. He could not have The Body, as she had been dubbed by the journalists, but he would always have the label. *When Fred Hollows was dying, Elle gave him a personally signed copy of her latest lingerie calendar ... an eyeful for the ophthalmologist ... Better get on with putting on my shirt ... Fred didn't fade. His light burned bright even in that last street of his life. Just like the lamps that snuffed themselves out as I approached them, in my dream, as if they were running away from me, the murderous me. Or is it me that's running away, that I just won't own the murder ...?*

Garrick remembered those words of his grandmother's, 'Never be afraid to dream, Garrick. Dream big, and always follow your dreams.'

But what about nightmares? Must we always follow those? And if those weren't true, why follow the others? Why pay any attention to dreams at all?

'Follow your dreams,' she used to say. 'Follow, wherever you they take you.'

Garrick ducked into the bathroom for a moment, to gaze at the mirror, finding himself suddenly in the grip of an urge to check that no angel had come to blaze the mark of Cain on his forehead, that his nightmare had not left him corporeally stigmatised. He thought of the blonde woman lying cold under the canvas sheet, black blood congealed at her open throat. He ached for Jade, bowed his head and prayed to the goddess on the wall, her face fixed in ecstasy on silver gelatine film, her dress blown up by the rollercoaster's rush. *Should I call her? What would I say? 'Hi honey, I'm just ringing to check you haven't been murdered?'* As Garrick climbed into his trousers, Picasso's *Le Pierrot* self-portrait on the opposing wall shook its head from side to side. *Is that picture really shaking its head at me? What a sad case I am! Perhaps it would've if it could.*

Garrick emerged from the bedroom, he picked up the remote and pointed it at the bench-top stereo. The Kinks picked up where they had left off, halfway through *Death of a Clown*.

Scenes from Gus Van Sant's *My Own Private Idaho* flashed through Garrick's mind as he ground two scoops of coffee plunger-fine and switched on the electric kettle. Cumulus clouds, tinged ochre-red, billowed in a cobalt sky as the tarmac rolled through the desert to a point where the haze at the horizon's edge bisected the frame. In a roadside motel, Hans the salesman danced with a bedside lamp, a gothic burlesque to smooth Keanu Reeves' and epileptic River Phoenix's hustle of the thieves.

Garrick's wandering mind sought out the roots of the scene, perhaps, in Dostoyevsky's *The Idiot*, in which another epileptic fool had loved a man intent on the assassination of love. Sipping coffee, Garrick flipped back through his notebook to the draft that was his own take on the theme, written the day he couldn't stop himself from staring at that woman with the long dark hair, the one in the red tartan miniskirt, sitting with her legs crossed, on the other side of the courtyard at Café Babylon. It had been a Saturday afternoon, the January before last. He'd scribbled a sonnet out on a piece of scrap paper, went up to her table to present it, turned bright red and left it with her

She giggled, stood up, turned her back to him and walked off towards the ladies' room. Then he fled.

Back at his unit, Garrick nursed his shame, painstakingly reconstructing the poem:

The Idiot

Bewitched, Prince Leo Nikolayevich
Myshkin, last and poorest of a line
of noblemen, stares across the room
at her tattooed shoulder, gripped by the itch
to approach her. Nastasya Filippovna gulps her wine
and glances back at him across the room.
Gripped by a fit by the throat in its garrotte,
he falls to the floor and froths, the idiot!

By the time that he comes to, she's gone
and he is lying in his own shit.
After the seizure, his state of mind is one
of insight and shame. (He'll get over it.)
He knows he wants to tell her she has better
tatts than Tank Girl, so he writes her a letter.

The sense of mastery achieved by writing this draft imploded on Monday morning when the woman from the café joined his ward round, long black hair plaited and secured with a ribbon, tattoos and thighs neatly covered by her modest blue uniform. She introduced herself as Rachel Flanaghan, the new clinical nurse consultant, fresh from Toronto.

*

Nick Myshkin turned up on time for his EEG that morning. Nick even lay down on the couch when he was told, and it was only when he asked the nurse, 'What the fuck has sticking paper dots with wires on my chest got to do with measuring my brain waves?' that the mistake was realised, so he was spared an unnecessary electrocardiogram. The nurse made a call up to the neurology laboratory and negotiated for the test to go ahead, even though he was half an hour late for it. She insisted on sticking Nick in a wheel chair, calling a wardsman, and personally escorting him to check in at Electroencephalography.

She's not such a bad sort, really. But this place is as bad as Fawlty Towers! Nick wondered what motivated people to be genuinely helpful. *He was not like that.* Are they going to wire me up to look like a Dalek? Seems that way, from the rubber cap that Asian bloke in the white coat is waving at me! Shit a brick! It's Wah-wah Bui! 'What the fuck are you doing here, Bui?'

'Hi, Nick, I'm the nurse technician here. I'll be setting you up for your EEG today. It's my day job. Come and sit over here. Be my guest! It's kinda funny, having you here. Fun and games ... Maybe you learn to pay on time, some day?'

Nick got up and walked across to the blue vinyl reclining chair. *Fuck a duck! Bui, here, whose Dad owns the club in Vulture Street. And I still owe his cut. As if he'd ever forget ...*

Hoa continued his orientation speech. 'Dr Willis is over there on the other side of the glass screen. He'll be watching you on the video monitor and checking your trace as it comes out on his computer screen in there. He'll tell me what he wants me to do when we come to the photic stimulation.'

'What the hell is that?'

In his left hand, Hoa held a white hair net with nobs on it. This was the Dalek hat Nick had already seen. That wasn't worrying him so much as the thing in Hoa's right hand, the hand that he'd held behind his back when he first came in and bent over Nick, peering at his coiffe with a gaze that Nick misread as emanating from a position of fierce disapproval, or else from one of alien detachment.

'You mean this?' Hoa enquired, brandishing the black plastic thing that looked a bit like a hair dryer and a lot like a ray gun. 'That's for drying the gel and fixing your coiffe back in place after we've finished.'

Nick had a lot of trouble telling when Asians were joking, and when they meant business. Especially this guy. *A mean bastard, but really good at keeping a straight face. So fucking inscrutable!*

'Don't look so worried!' said Hoa, now breaking into a broad grin, which Nick found even more confusing. 'I hope you can take a joke! It gets very boring in here setting up for these tests every day. Sometimes I like to play a little. It's the photic stimulator!'

'And I'm supposed to find that reassuring?' Bui was the kind of guy who only turns up at church so he can try out his joy buzzer when he shakes hands with the preacher.

'When Dr Willis gives me the signal, I will point the gun into your eyes, and a stroboscopic laser beam will be projected through this vent, a bright blue flashing light. Sometimes that can cause some people to have a fit, or maybe just to space out a little. I will watch your behaviour and report back to Dr Willis what I see. I'll keep the flashing light going for about one minute, while he watches the EEG trace on his monitor screen.'

'So you're going to use that to try to make me have a fit?'

'Yes, you could say that! It's better to find it out here, now, okay? Better than if it happens next time a strobe comes on when you're out clubbing, or when the screen flickers on the television, or when you're driving and the sunlight flickers in and out through a paling fence. All these things sometimes trigger people to have fits. In some situations that can be very dangerous.'

He's not so inscrutable now. This bastard's loving every minute of this.

Hoa put the ray gun down on the bench, continued to hold the rubber cap in his left hand and picked up a squeeze bottle of with the jubilant bee logo on the label.

'Hey, that's honey! What are you going to do with that shit?'

'I'm going to squirt it on to special places on your scalp. It helps to give a better reading. And besides, it helps the cap stay on!'

Really? When am I supposed to take this guy seriously?

'But I don't know what we're going to do about that mighty coiffe!'

'You leave that alone! You're not touching it!'

'Whoa! Easy now! No need to get all het up and shirty with me!' Hoa was struggling with the net cap now, trying to pull to on over the unicorn horn that Nick had made out of his hair.

'Careful! You'll break the gel!' Nick jerked his head away from Hoa's hands.

Hoa shrugged and said, 'I don't know what to do.' Then, scratching his head: 'I suppose I could cut a hole in it, and let the coiffe poke out. You OK with that?'

'Yeah, sure. Give it a shot.'

Hoa picked up a pair of scissors and cut away at the netting at the front of the cap. He then eased the net along the horn of Nick's coiffe from the pointy end, cutting a little more as he went, allowing the hole to become sufficiently wide to allow Nick's solid gelled stalk to poke through without interference. Then he pulled the net over Nick's crown.

Looking pretty smug now, aren't you, you little prick!

Hoa went over to turn on the contraption connected to the lead coming out of the back of the hairnet cap, then walked to the other machine, just to the right of Nick's chair, and pushed the start button. The brushes began to trace wave patterns as the roll of graph paper began to move.

Nick asked, 'How does that thing trace my brain waves when it's not connected to the cap?'

'Each of the knobs in the cap is a radio transmitter with an electrode on the end near your scalp, picking up the electrical activity over the part of your brain beneath it. These signals are transmitted to the receiver in this machine over here, and then converted into movements of the arms that put the ink onto this paper trace. The computer that sends the signal to the arms is also sending signals to the monitor Dr Willis is watching next door. First he wants a resting trace. Now I'm going to give you a few simple commands to follow. I will signal to Dr Willis when each action starts and stops by pushing this button. Now close your eyes and screw them up tight! That's good. You can relax and open your eyes again now. Now poke out your tongue and hold. That's good. Relax again now! Now clench your teeth and grind them! Yes, that's good. Now relax!' Hoa spoke into the microphone protruding from his headset. 'Dr Willis, was that all okay?'

'Yes, Hoa, that's all good!'

Nick jumped when Garrick's voice came out of the speaker in the wall.

'What was that?' asked Garrick.

'I think you frightened him!'

'Hello, Nick! Sorry to scare you. How are you doing?'

'Well, this is all a bit weird, but I'm all right I guess.'

'Has Hoa told you about the photic stimulation?'

'Yeah, after he waved his ray gun around for a while!'

'And are you okay with that?'

'What if I have a fit?'

'I'll ask Hoa to put in a rubber mouth guard with an air hole in it before we do the next bit. And put a butterfly needle into the back of your hand. We've got some Valium drawn up over there on the bench. If you start to fit, I'll watch here for a little while so we get a trace, then I'll pop in on you after a few seconds and inject the Valium to stop it. We might need to keep you here for a couple of hours observation if that happens. Shall we go ahead?'

'Yeah, all right, Doc, but this is all pretty weird.'

Hoa had put on rubber gloves while Garrick was speaking with Nick. He brought the mouthpiece in a silver kidney dish, picked it up and asked Nick to open wide as he inserted it. He went to the bench and picked up the ray gun again. 'Right to go now, Doc?'

'Ready, Nick?' asked Garrick-who-lived-in-the-speaker.

'It's hard to talk with this thing in my mouth, but hit me with all you've got, Mr Spaceman!'

Hoa raised the stroboscope, pointed it at Nick's face and squeezed the trigger. Flashing waves of bright blue light came out of the broad end of the barrel, the part that made it look so much like a hair dryer.

Nick looked bewildered for a moment. Then his eyes began flicking rapidly towards the left, drifting back more slowly to the right each time. Air hissed from the hole in the mouthpiece. Nick's eyes closed, his jaws clamped, his back stiffened and arched, his fingers clenched into fists and his toes curled under. Then his whole body began to jerk and twitch spasmodically.

Hoa had seen this many times in response to photic stimulation, but not usually so rapidly, or so dramatically. A patch of moisture spread out from the front of Nick's gown. Hoa was glad he had placed an absorbent pad on the seat. He wondered how long Garrick would let this go on.

Garrick-on-the-other-side-of-the-screen watched the monitors. The seizure activity had first shown itself on the trace from the left temporal electrode, but very rapidly spread throughout both cerebral hemispheres. The trace showed all the electrodes generating huge spike and wave patterns, and via the direct observation monitor, Garrick could see that the patient was having a full-on grand mal seizure. It had gone on long enough to be diagnostically conclusive, so it was time to stop it. Garrick got up from his chair and opened the door in the glass screen. 'Valium 10mg, please!'

Hoa looked sheepish.

'Don't tell me you've forgotten to draw it up!' At times like this, Garrick was prone to wonder what had destined him to work surrounded by idiots.

By the time Garrick returned to the ward for his round, Nick was wide awake, chatting with Rachel Flanaghan.

Rachel bent from the waist to feel Nick's forehead. 'I'd better take your temperature. You're a little hot!'

'Not half as hot as you, nurse,' said Nick.

'That's enough of that, you cheeky man!'

Strange, thought Garrick, that she should be so flirty with Nick, after having to clean him up after the EEG fiasco. Does she know him from somewhere else? What would a girl like Rachel see in a deadbeat like Nick?

Garrick beckoned Rachel to leave the bedside and, just outside the curtain, whispered to her, 'Did you notice anything strange as he was coming round?'

'He just kept muttering "Sorry, Jade!" or something like that.'

Garrick was troubled. He returned to the bedside with the nurse and asked Nick, 'How's it going now?'

'A bit of a headache, Doc. And I'm aching all over, like I'm been hit by a truck. What happened? I must've been out for a while?'

'Well, the photic stimulation brought on a fit, a full grand mal seizure. You lost consciousness, your muscles tensed up, then your whole body began jerking. I had to rush in from next door and give you an injection of Valium to stop it, to make sure you didn't come to any serious harm.'

'So I really had a full-on fit, Doc?'

'Yes, you did. You definitely have epilepsy, Nick. So we must start you on tablets to prevent more fits. If you'll stay until tomorrow, we'll give you a loading dose of Epilim tonight, and be able to make a fair guess at a regular dose to discharge you on tomorrow morning. You'll need to have a test to check the level of the drug in your blood in five days, and I'll see you again at my clinic next week. I'll have the results back by then, so we can adjust the dose. It might take a few weeks to get the levels into the right range for you.' Garrick turned to Rachel and asked 'What does he weigh?'

'Seventy-five kilograms, Dr Willis.'

'Thanks, Sister.' Garrick was having those thoughts again. He hoped he wasn't turning pink and flushing all over. 'We'll give him a stat dose of a gram tonight, and start him on 400mg twice daily for discharge tomorrow.' He turned to Rachel, 'Make sure you book him into my Thursday clinic.'

'As good as done, Dr Willis!'

'And what are the side effects, Doc?' asked Nick, just as Garrick turned his back on him and moved in the direction of the next bed.

Garrick's iPhone rang, sounding the theme from *The Twilight Zone*. His father's mobile number appeared on the screen. He turned back to Nick and said, 'Sorry, I must take this call. Dr Sorensen will tell you more about the medication. I'll see you in clinic, Thursday next week. Don't forget to go to pathology and have the blood test done on Monday. In the morning, before you take your tablet.' *The Twilight Zone* continued to wail in the background until Garrick took the call. He stepped out into the corridor and began striding towards the lifts, holding the phone to his ear. 'Hello, Dad?'

'Hi Garrick, I know you're busy, but your Grandma's had another stroke, and she's in a bad way.'

'That's terrible..'

'Dr Throsby's put her in St Vincent's. She can't walk, talks a lot of rubbish and one side of her face is numb. She's had a fall and broke her arm, too. They can't operate to fix it unless they stop the drugs that prevent the strokes for at least a week.'

'No, they can't operate on her while that stuff's in her system. She'd bleed to death. Poor Grandma.'

'Old Throsby says she'll probably die before then if they do, but he said the surgeon would like to talk to you before we make a decision.'

'Ok, Dad, I will.'

'I've got Mum's Power of Attorney, but your Aunty Charlie's upset and can't take it in. We'd really appreciate your help down here, son. And your Grandma's been calling out for you. Can you make it down?'

'I'm supposed to knock off at 5.00, but I'll tell the juniors to cover for me. I'd better talk to Jade and grab a few things from home. By the time I've done that, it'll be 4.30. So I'll get to Lismore around seven tonight, and see you up at St Vincent's then.'

'Yeah, well, come and have a beer and stay over with us. It's about time we caught up.'

'All right, Dad. See you soon.'

*

When Garrick arrived at St Vincent's, a crowd had gathered around Grandma Edie. The Baptist pastor had just left, and various members of the family were talking all at once without turn-taking, one over the top of the other. Aunty Charlie sat beside the bed spitting out a monologue on Edie's movements over the past week. She hugged Garrick and said, 'Grandma was looking forward to the holiday at Caloundra. Holden and I booked it for a fortnight's time. We were going to take her away for a few days.'

Don, Garrick's dad, a grey-haired and tanned with weathered skin, still on the kinder side of sixty, wiped his hand on his khaki builder's overalls before taking Garrick's and shaking it, saying, 'Good to see you, son! Glad you could make it.'

Aunty Charlie broke in again, interpreting the groan that came out of Grandma's throat after a belch when Garrick entered the room as: 'Mum's way of letting us know that she was pleased to see her doctor grandson'.

Garrick walked to the right-hand side of the bed and took his grandmother's hand.

'She knows you're there, Garrick! She's been waiting for you. That's why she's hung on. She'd been calling for you. She knew you were coming.'

Don raised his eyebrows and nodded in his wife's, Christine's, direction. Garrick had never quite known what to call her. But she'd been good for Don, and apart from Grandma, the closest thing he and his sister Sandy had known to a real mum. Mother was a word that was fuzzy for Garrick, fuzzy and confusing. Which one should he call Mum? He knew he loved his Grandma, and that Christine had treated him with greater kindness and warmth than he'd ever known from Charmaine, his birth mother. Not that he even knew where Charmaine was these days. The last he'd heard of her she'd been doing rehab with the Salvos, in a place surrounded by banana farms, somewhere up in the hills near Cobaki.

Aunty Charlie chattered on, offering a high-pitched racing commentary. Garrick remembered Grandma being like that when Grandpa was dying. It'd been hard to get a word in edgeways, even just to say goodbye to the old man. Mercifully, Christine interrupted Charlie in the middle of a recitation of the old lady's last shopping list. 'Come on, Charlie, let me take you for a coffee, you've been here all day with her and up all night too. You need a break.'

Garrick shook his shoulders to release the tension and let out a sigh as his stepmother shepherded Aunty Charlie out of the room.

Charlie's husband Holden followed.

He's like a handbag, Garrick thought to himself. He was glad that his Dad stayed behind in the room, as did Aunty Alison and Uncle Phil. Garrick wondered about Uncle Ray, whom he hadn't seen for a year or two. Ray was just a few years older than him, much younger than Dad. Three years younger than Phil. Somehow Ray seemed more like an older brother to Garrick, whereas Phil seemed like part of Dad's generation, even though there were more than ten years between Phil and Don. Ray had probably been in earlier, and most likely was now working on the evening shift as nurse in charge of the surgical emergency theatre up at Lismore Hospital. Garrick knew that he had been the last to come, except for his sister Sandy, who was still on the way from Dubai, probably in the air by now. No one expected Grandma to last this one out. Garrick agreed with Khan, the orthopaedic surgeon he'd spoken with briefly on the phone before taking the drive down. Grandma would need to have the Plavix out of her system at least a week for safe surgery. By then she'd probably be gone.

Grandma seemed awfully quiet. If she was breathing at all, her breath was shallow and slow. Her left arm was shortened at the shoulder, held in a splint, and lying across her chest in a sling. Just the same, the intravenous line had been inserted in the back of her left hand. The IVAC quietly monitored the flow of dextrose and saline from the bag on the stand and into her veins. The second line, Garrick guessed, must be the morphine infusion. That smaller bag was nearly empty. Garrick had Grandma's good hand in his right. Gently, he felt for her pulse and was relieved to find it—weak and irregular, with lots of dropped beats, but a pulse is a pulse. Grandma was still with them. Then he got up, went to the foot of the bed and uncovered her feet. He drew his car key from his pocket and ran it up the outside of the soles of each of her feet, from the heel to the toes. No reaction. Grandma was either brain dead, or else the morphine had put her so deep that even her reflexes had gone to sleep.

None of the others, not Phil, nor Alison, and certainly not Don, dared to ask Garrick for an explanation. He returned to the side of Edie Guyton's bed and took her right hand again, gently and tenderly, in his. Garrick bent low over his grandmother's face and kissed her cheek, then lowered himself into the seat again and tried to speak, but found that his body wrenched with the first of a series of violent sobs. The tears began to flow down his cheeks. His nose was pouring snot. He hadn't cried like this since he was seven, when his fox terrier pup had slipped out of her collar and run in front of a truck.

Don stepped forward and put his arm around his son's shoulder. Garrick accepted the embrace, but didn't turn to see. If he had, he would have found his father's leather cheeks were just as wet, but Don's way of showing it was quieter.

'Follow your dreams, boy. Never be afraid to dream,' Grandma had said.

Maybe it was that he shook the bed as he sobbed, jolting her broken arm and waking up the pain. Garrick rattled and gasped out his gratitude and grief—as he struggled to say 'Thank you so much Grandma for everything you've done. You've taught me what it is to love, and I love you so much. I don't want to say it, but I'm glad I've gotten here while you're still alive, so I can say goodbye'.

The old lady stirred and opened her eyes, looked into his, gurgled and appeared to be struggling to speak. Then a pained look came over her face. Her legs kicked and thrashed. Then her eyes closed, and she was still again. 'Dad,' said Garrick, 'I think we'd better call the nurse. Grandma needs more morphine.'

Just then the IVAC began to beep. Alison peered at the bag and confirmed, 'It's empty.'

The nurse, a brawny redheaded country girl with arms thicker than Garrick's thighs, came in and set up a new bag for the infusion. As she was finishing, Christine brought Aunty Charlie and Uncle Holden back.

Charlie looked exhausted, yet the machine-gun chattered on. Holden remained quieter than the unmarked grave that was the fate of any soldier who might cross her.

'It's getting late,' said the nurse. 'You folks look like you've been through the wringer. But you're not going to do any good here tonight. When that shot runs through, Mrs Guyton's gonna need her rest, and so you'd best go home and get some too. We'll call you if she looks like she's gonna slip away, but I'd say that won't be tonight, and tomorrow's gonna be another big day for you, so go and have your dinner and we'll watch over her.'

'Thanks, Sister,' said Garrick and led the way out the door. The others filed after him, with his Dad and Christine having to drag Charlie out, one on each arm, while Holden guarded the rear.

HIS MOTHER'S BODY

Garrick spent the night at Dad's place up on the hill at Goonellabah, not far from Grandma's house at East Lismore, where he slept in a cot for the first weeks of his life, before Dad and Charmaine found a place of their own. When Charmaine left and Dad went off to work in the mines, he and Sandy stayed with Grandma. Dad's room had been his room then. He was glad not to have to be there tonight. If he slept in that bed, the old nightmares would return, and maybe the ghosts as well.

At least at Dad's place, Garrick thought, *I won't hear graves being dug outside the window.* After about half an hour of tossing and turning, he drifted off. The dream came anyway, as it had before. Garrick came across the entrance to a tunnel in a hillside, with Chinese pictograms across the lintel. He stepped into the darkness, somehow seeing just enough to make his way without a torch. The tunnel kept branching, this way and that.

Garrick heard his grandmother's voice calling, 'Follow your dreams, Garrick, follow your dreams.'

He tried to walk with confidence, first following the left hand fork, then the right. The walls of the tunnel were elastic, expanding and contracting, beating and booming in time with his heart. Panic crept upon him, terror at being lost. Then he emerged into a cemetery where someone arrived in a long black hearse, the coffin decked out with pink and white gladioli. He'd missed the service at the church and must sneak around the periphery, lest he be caught. Then he woke with his sheets knotted and soaked with sweat. That dream came back to him, even here.

Garrick was up at 3.30 a.m. with the light on in the kitchen, scribbling into his notebook, crossing out lines and scribbling over them again.

Down the tunnel of fear, I follow, through the Chinese cemetery
inside my mother's body, where the drum of the heart beats hollow
as the gong and the kookaburra choir of a sunburnt country laughs
at my longing for the silk-seamed calves of the femme fatale from film
noir.

The kitchen clock showed 4.30 a.m. That fragment was the best Garrick could do for now. He got up and turned the light off on the way back to bed, where he lay awake as the dawn struggled to penetrate the open slats of the blinds. Around 5.00 a.m. the kookaburras in the bloodwoods on the vacant lot next door began to laugh, at him, not with him.

Garrick gave up on sleep, got out of bed, put on his robe, picked up his toiletry bag and headed for the bathroom. After a shower and shave, he dressed and made himself coffee and toast. He left a thank you note for Dad and Christine, and drove back to Brisbane for Tuesday's work.

*

Don called Garrick again at 11.00 the following Thursday morning, just as Garrick was about to do his neurology ward round at Logan Hospital.

Garrick tried to fool himself that there wasn't a messianic bone in his body—or if there was, he'd had it surgically removed, then deposited it when the offering plate came round during his annual Christmas ritual, taking Grandma to worship at the Lismore Baptist Church, while Dad and Christine stayed home making prawn cocktails and baking the turkey. On Logan days he felt like Jesus must've after a hard day out healing the sick, then trying to convince the apostles to remain optimistic about the prospect of feeding five thousand people from a parcel of five bake-at-home dinner rolls and two small whiting.

The call interrupted the Persian registrar's unsympathetic presentation of a middle-aged Cambodian woman with a debilitating case of *tic dolereux*—chronic facial pain—and oral opioid addiction. Garrick still found it surprising when successful refugees from oppression looked down on those who hadn't done so well. *I should restrain myself from suggesting that a childhood spent in Pol Pot's killing camp, and the memory of watching her baby sister torn from her mother's breast and swung by the heels until her head smashed against the banyan tree in the yard of a desecrated temple might have something to do with her ending up the way she is.*

But the Khmer interpreter was doing the job for him, and that the teaching method most commonly used on him in medical school— public humiliation—was the wrong one. He also wondered, if Dr Amirzedeh had the opportunity to present the patient's history in Farsi, would the kindness of his heart's regard have been more readily apparent? Perhaps it was just as well that his father's call came then, milking venom from the glands under the neurologist's tongue.

The Twilight Zone persistently sounded from Garrick's phone. He excused himself to the patient and the interpreter, leaving Dr

Amirzedeh to carry on. In the corridor, he pressed the answer button. His father's voice came down the line.

'Your Grandma, Garrick, she's gone.'

'I'm so sorry to hear that, Dad. She seemed to be getting back from it.'

'She made a massive recovery from that stroke, didn't she? It was seeing you that brought her back. You were her favourite grandchild. You know that?'

'Did she say that?'

'Yes, son. She was so proud of you. And she always said, "Let him follow his dreams." She rallied after you came to see her that night. She did all right with the surgery, too. Might've been home in a few more days if it hadn't been for the blood clot in her leg. They were just about to start the Plavix again. She had the clot, in spite of them wrapping her up in those big white stockings. Then, the next thing, it went straight to her lungs. In the early hours, this morning. When the pain came, she was gripping my hand and looking up at me with those pale blue eyes. Reminded me of Lou Reed singing that song with Velvet Underground back in the sixties, when I was just out of school. The pain in those eyes. And now she's gone. Half an hour ago.'

'How was it at the end?'

'I told them that we didn't want to see her suffer anymore, and she wouldn't want to linger on. So they gave her a big shot of morphine. Aunty Charlie and I were there when she closed those eyes for the last time. She's seen a lot through those eyes, a lot of pain, son. And she's always been there for us. But she's gone now. At least she went peacefully. I couldn't see her suffer any more, knowing all that she's been through.'

Garrick heard his father struggling over the words, to be manly, to not break down and cry. Not that Don would think that's what made a man a man. He was brought up was to have a tender heart, but watch your back, and be careful who is watching any time you show weakness. 'I'm so sorry, Dad. You did the right thing. It's a bit of a shock to me though, too. Grandma's always been there. I guess when I saw her last, she looked as if she wouldn't make it, and so I let go of her then. But I didn't give her credit for being so tough. She made it through to surgery, with some hope of going home. She never would've coped in a nursing home, Dad. She had to have the surgery. It was always going to be a risk. But she took the chance. Funny, though. It will take me a while to get used to her not being there. Somehow I thought that maybe she could live forever.'

'Yeah, she was a fighter, son. She sure fought for us kids after my Dad died and she was left with us ... Anyway, the funeral's set for Monday. She's arranged it all in advance, written everything down in a little pink book. She told Charlie that she wants you to do the eulogy.'

Garrick gulped. 'Are you sure, Dad? Wouldn't she have left that to Uncle Phil? He's almost qualified as a minister.'

'No, she was absolutely clear with Charlie. She said: "My grandson, Garrick the doctor, will speak at my funeral. You can all help him tell my story. I've written all the dates and places in this book. I don't want that biker son of mine, Phillip, thinking he can tell all the dirt on me just because he's been to Bible College. Garrick will do a nice job of it. He's got a good speaking voice. And he can write poetry." So I guess you've got the job, son, and we'll be expecting you to give it your best. When can you come down again?'

'Well, Dad, I guess I'm writing the eulogy. I'll take a couple of days of bereavement leave. I'll come down tonight and have tomorrow and the weekend to work on it with the family around to help me.'

'And are you going to bring that fast lady nurse of yours with you this time? Reminds me of your mother. You've got to be careful with that one, son. But I will say this, she's certainly got your mum's body.'

*

Waiting for the train at Meadowbrook Station, Garrick was thinking of his afternoon patient list. Nick Myshkin would be seeing him again. *Surely Nick wouldn't be on the train with me, again? He wouldn't be coming this way. Didn't he live at West End? Or was it somewhere over at New Farm? I'd rather not see him anywhere outside of the clinic. And I'm not too fond of seeing him there, either.*

On the way to Dutton Park, Garrick ran through a series of mental pictures of Grandma at the different times of his life. Who really was his mother? Grandma had certainly been more of a mother to him than Charmaine, but even Christine had done better for him. And she'd been so much better for Dad.

When Garrick made it back the Princess, Nick Myshkin was already there in the waiting room. Garrick read the list again—just Myshkin and one other, a bus driver with Gilles de la Tourette syndrome. Mercifully, the verbal tics were rare, and a milligram of risperidone a day seemed to keep the motor tics at bay, with less severe side effects than when he'd tried haloperidol. Best of all, now that unfortunate man was virtually cured, he often forgot to come to his appointments. Today though, he had rung to cancel, just an hour before. *If only Nick had stayed away as well.* Garrick picked up the file and called Nick Myshkin in.

'How's it going, Doc? You're looking a bit down. Like a dog's breakfast?'

'I'm fine, thanks,' snapped Garrick. 'I don't seem to have your blood test results?'

'I forgot until this morning. Then I went in and couldn't have the test anyway, because I had already taken my tablet.'

That's something, anyway, thought Garrick. At least he's taking them. Better than I'd expected. 'Any trouble with the tablets?'

'I was a bit groggy in the morning, the day after I left hospital. And a bit queasy in the belly. But no trouble since then.'

'Any more fits, or faints, or funny turns?'

'No, Doc! I've actually felt clearer in my head since the fit that happened when you were doing the EEG test with the ray gun. I don't know if that's the tablets?'

'It might be, but it's more probably just the fit itself, at this stage. Until you've had the blood test, I can't know whether or not you're on an adequate dose. I expect I'll have to put it up, once we know the levels. But there's no better protection against fits than having a huge fit like the one you did when you were in hospital. It stabilises the nerve cell membranes in a way that regulates the brain's electrical activity. Often patients report greater clarity of thought and improved mood for months after a really good fit. And at least we confirmed the diagnosis.'

'You sound like Ian Drury from The Blockheads, listing *Reasons To Be Cheerful.*'

'Well, there's always plenty to be cranky about if we go looking for it. I'd better write you a new prescription. If you get that test done tomorrow, I can get you back to clinic next week again, so we can adjust the dose.'

Garrick wrote out the script and handed it to Nick, who pulled his wallet out of the back pocket of his jeans, intending to stuff the thing in there with the bank notes. He dropped the wallet at Garrick's feet. It landed with the photo page open. Garrick bent to pick it up, and noticed that the shot was of a Slavic man on a big bike, and a woman with long black hair trailing back, holding the man's waist tight as she straddled the pillion, her boots on the pegs, leather skirt riding up to show her thighs wrapped round his. A wild ecstatic expression on her face, she turned to the camera, slightly blurred by speed. Scribbled across it, in a strangely familiar hand: 'Leo and Charmaine, 1975.'

Garrick felt a tingle run down his spine, as if something weird was happening. He felt compelled to say, 'You know, we could almost be brothers' as he passed over the wallet.

Nick grinned as he took it, then reached to shake Garrick's hand.

My mother's body, Garrick thought, *wrapped around a Ruskie on a Harley?*

PALE BLUE EYES

In the dream, Garrick was seventeen again, his slender body in the blue and gold uniform of the Lismore Athletics Club, running down a moonlit pathway between the monuments on the hill in the North Lismore Memorial Rest Park, where the tombstones had been removed in the sixties and lined up in tight little rows looking down on the newly anonymous graves of those under the green field below. As he passed the cross of William Steenson, the one famous for its eerie glow, a tall gangly figure in a long brown robe jumped out from behind the stone. A quick look over his right shoulder gave him a view of the creature's face—Garrick's own face, but with pale blue luminescent eyes, a drooling snarl and fangs. Garrick's hair, at that age, had been thick and sun-bleached, growing down beyond his collar. The creature's hair was longer, streaming out behind him like a pennant in the wind as he ran. The doppelgänger's stride matched Garrick's, and then some, so that it was slowly gaining on him, barefoot, seeming unimpeded by its cassock covered in magic symbols sewn on to the coarse burnt-umbre cloth in patches of woven gold.

It was at Garrick's shoulder, running on his shadow, but it cast none. Soon it would overtake him, and take him over. At this thought, a rage rose in him that was greater than his fear. He spun around to face the thing, his back to the crest of the hill, taking the stance he instinctively assumed when attacked in the streets by a dog on the loose, knees bent and feet planted wide apart, hands up in front, ready to grapple. The creature howled as it leapt towards him, flying through the air to connect with the shoe at the end of Garrick's well aimed solar plexus kick. Doubled up and shrieking with pain, the creature torpedoed in the trajectory of the boot. Up, up and over the moon, never to be seen again.

*

Strange, thought Garrick, that he should dream that dream again here the night before Grandma's funeral. He woke feeling exhilarated, relieved, alive, as he would after coming out on top from a great physical ordeal. He remembered feeling like that after he'd broken the record in the school cross country, and when his club soccer team had won the grand final that same year. But also liberated. Then apprehensive, realising he had turned his back on something vital, repudiated some essential part of himself. That dream had been the last nightmare he'd had before finishing school and leaving home to study medicine in Brisbane.

Nothing much had troubled him after that, not until he encountered gross anatomical dissection in the second year. He had shared the task with five other students, all of them gathered around a stainless steel table, ridged drains at the sides, three students to each side. He and his friend Melissa *(where was she now? Working for the WHO, running a hospital for AIDS orphans somewhere in Africa?)* had worked on the lower limbs and the pelvis. Sometimes the flirting across the table was intense. The cadaver had been a big heavy-set old woman who'd reminded him too much of Grandma. He'd come home to College in the evenings stinking of formalin and then have to face the meat concoction on his plate in the dining room, smelling and looking much the same as what he'd left on the slab.

77

For a while after that, Garrick found himself unable to dream. Or at least he didn't remember them. Except when he came home on holidays. Except when he slept in this room.

Garrick reached out to put his right arm over Jade's waist, and slipped his left arm under her. She'd swapped out of a late shift to make it down last night, so she could stay on for the funeral. He stroked her belly and played with the golden dragonfly he'd bought when she had her navel pierced. She tucked into him so nicely when he wrapped himself around her. He began to poke at her and tickle with what seemed to him, after a dream like that, to be a surprisingly huge boner.

*

Having been with Grandma when she died, and knowing what state Aunt Charlie would be in, Don and Christine had decided not to attend the viewing, so Garrick drove Sandy over to the Parkview Funeral Home, just a few streets away, where the Szeliski boys had laid Grandma out in the dress that she had worn on the day of Garrick's marriage to Penny.

Jade came along for the ride, but decided to stay in the car. *Only once met the old girl once, so why attend the viewing?*

Garrick took his sister's hand, and they walked together through the door to reception. The duty manager showed them to the viewing room. Grandma looked very peaceful. Those Szeliski boys had done a good job. The older one taught Sunday School at Lismore Baptist when Garrick was a boy, and the younger one had been in the year ahead of Garrick at Lismore High. He played soccer with Garrick's club. Come to think of it, he dated Sandy once or twice before she went away to do her information technology degree at Armidale. They'd been fond of Grandma and gotten used to her regular attendance at so many of the funerals they'd run, in her unofficial role as chief mourner for the Lismore branch of the Women's Christian Temperance Union. Even in death, they treated her well. Soon the duty manager would close the lid on Grandma forever, screw it down tight, and call for assistance to wheel her round to the chapel, ready for the 11.00 a.m. service.

Garrick held Sandy tight as they approached the coffin. Yes, Sandy had her mother's long black hair. And Grandma's pale blue eyes. They were beginning to water. He took Grandma's cold hand in his, and leant to gently kiss her on the cheek. Sandy did the same.

Then Garrick looked up at Sandy and said, 'Do you remember when Grandma was really cranky, she'd threaten to send me away to boarding school, and sometimes even to send me to Boystown?'

'Yes,' said Sandy. 'I do. And she used to threaten to sell me to the Arabs!'

*

After the viewing, Garrick and Sandy interrupted Jade fixing her make up in the Beemer's rear view mirror.

Garrick started the engine, and took them for a short drive over to Grandma's house, where he stood in silence for a while under the macadamia tree in the left front corner of the yard. He bent down to pick something up and put it in the right inside breast pocket of his charcoal grey suit. He checked in the left breast pocket, reassured himself that the eulogy was there, then walked around to the back yard where Sandy was wandering about, gazing at this tree, and that vine, and especially at the dilapidated set of swings, with the chains rusting. A bud on one of Grandma's rose bushes, a dark pink one, was just beginning to open. Garrick reached down and took the stem in his hands, thorns and all, broke it off and handed it to Sandy. *The shine in those blue eyes of hers is truly remarkable.*

Jade scowled at him, dipped into her purse, pulled out a lighter and lit up a cigarette.

Sandy pinned the rose to the lapel of her jacket. 'You've made yourself bleed,' she said to Garrick, looking at the spots on his palm where the thorns had pricked him. She pulled a tissue out of her purse and handed it to him. He clenched on it.

'Reminds me that I'm still alive,' he said.

Garrick drove back to the chapel, which was beginning to fill for the service.

Uncle Phil roared into the drive on his Ducati Streetfighter 848, wearing full leathers with the God's Squad Northern New South Wales chapter patch on the back of his jacket. He took off his helmet and opened the right side pannier, fishing for his Bible. Phil hung about outside. He didn't immediately follow them into the chapel.

Garrick took a seat beside his father in the second row. Sandy sat next to Christine, on the other side of Don. He found himself looking around for Charmaine, although he knew she wouldn't be there. It wasn't that he missed her. It was just that at any important family event, something drove him to look for her, and to acknowledge to himself that she was absent. It was as if in some way, for him, her absence had come to be a kind of presence, one that had to be checked for and given its place, before anything could begin.

Aunty Alison, recently widowed, was sitting just in front of Garrick. Aunty Charlie held her hand, with the dutiful Holden beside her. Uncle Ray and his partner Günther came in and joined Alison, Charlie and Holden in the front pew. The other grandchildren, Garrick's cousins, filed into the couple of rows behind him. Great Aunt Jeanie, Great Uncle Doug, his wife, and all their families, as well as Great Uncle Ron's, sat in the front pews across the aisle way. Behind them, the chapel was full to overflowing with church people, and with those who'd known Grandpa Guyton through the TPI League, Legacy and the RSL.

Jade took her time finishing her cigarette. When she came in, she walked up to join the family and sat down on Garrick's right. Phil followed and planted himself next to her. With the Good Book in his left hand, Phillip reached across Jade to offer Garrick his hand. They shook. Garrick had never liked Phil, who was old enough to successfully torment him when they lived together at Grandma's house, but too immature to know better. Their eyes met as they shook hands. In spite of all that, it was hard to sustain his hatred of Phil when he too had Grandma's pale blue eyes.

EULOGY

Phil did not have his way. The senior pastor of the Lismore Baptist church presided over the funeral. Grandma had chosen all the hymns herself, some of which were not familiar to Reverend Anderson, who was left guessing as to what she'd meant. A number of those that were on offer were entirely unfamiliar to most of the congregation.

Phil had to settle for doing the reading Grandma had chosen from St Paul's second letter to the Corinthians. He read from the New International Version, although Mrs Guyton had been adamant that she wanted it from King James: 'But we have this treasure in jars of clay to show that the all-surpassing power of God is not from us. We are hard pressed on every side, but not crushed; perplexed, but not in despair; persecuted, but not abandoned; struck down, but not destroyed. We always carry around in our body the death of Jesus, so that the life of Jesus can be revealed in our body. So then, death is at work in our body, but life is at work in you.

'It is written: "I believed; therefore I have spoken." Since we have that same spirit of faith, we also believe and therefore speak, because we know the one who raised the Lord Jesus from the dead will also raise us with Jesus and present us with you to himself. All this is for your benefit, so the grace that is reaching more and more people may cause thanksgiving to overflow to the glory of God.

'Therefore we do not lose heart. For our light and momentary troubles are achieving us an eternal glory that outweighs them all. So we fix our eyes not on what is seen, but on what is unseen, since what is seen is temporary, but what is unseen is eternal.'

When Phil sat down, Ray Guyton rose from his seat and came to the microphone to sing one of Grandma's favourites, *The Old Rugged Cross*. Ray had a fine voice, but he was shaking with emotion, cracking on the high notes, and barely managed to hold together through the third verse. When Ray had finished, Reverend Anderson got up again and announced that Mrs Guyton's grandson, Dr Garrick Willis, would give an account of the life of Edith. Garrick stood, pushed past Jade and Phil to the aisle, walked up past the coffin, and came to the lectern to deliver the euology. Phil moved himself closer to Jade.

'My grandmother was a wild farm girl, riding a horse six miles every day to the Ironpot Creek State School. Great Uncle Ron told me all the boys were scared of fighting her. This was advantageous for him, his brother Douglas and his sister Jeanie, but there was also a downside to having a volatile older sister. One time, Edie brought a kerosene tin down on Great Uncle Doug's head. She was jealous of a gift from their grandmother, who'd granted Douglas exclusive access to a tin of condensed milk.

'Edie took no notice of her father's warning not to interfere with a shell-shocked warhorse he was breaking in. No sooner was Herb out of sight than she vaulted into the saddle and rode that skittish animal into a lather of sweat and foam, up and down the hillside, leaping over fences and whatever obstacles came their way, until the poor thing collapsed outside the stable. She copped a thrashing for that, as she did regularly for her own misdemeanours, and sometimes for those of her siblings as well.'

Garrick looked up. Jade was smiling at him, pouting her lips. Phil looked very pleased with himself.

Garrick struggled to keep his composure, but pushed on with stories of Grandma Edie's childhood in the Northern Rivers. He warned the congregation that, in such stories, 'Time and place blur and weave, coalesce and separate, twisting back on each other. You may become confused about names, and the tenuous web of interpersonal and intergenerational connections. That's the way time and place were for my grandmother, the way the stories she told us came out. Grandma stayed at school only to the seventh grade, although she was later proud to achieve her intermediate elocution certificate. She went to work on her parents' farm, feeding the animals, milking the cows. But by her late teens, she was dying to get away from it.

'It may not surprise those of you who knew Edie for the horsewoman she once was—my grandmother had a thing for men on motorcycles! When a young man named Athol Willis came courting on his Harley Davidson, he took Grandma for the ride of their lives. They married when she was 18 and Athol was 21, and a year or so later, my eldest aunty Alison was born, followed two years later by Charlene, and after another four years, by my father Donald.

'Athol managed Hogan's saw mill efficiently. My grandmother kept the books and allocated the men's wages, in addition to her duties at home.

'Unfortunately, this happy time was cut short by the poliomyelitis epidemic of 1953. Athol took sick suddenly, and died four days later in an iron lung in Lismore Base Hospital. By the time Edie was allowed to enter the isolation ward to say goodbye, Athol was already unconscious. He passed away as she waited out on the hospital verandah. She went home to her parents' Oliver Avenue house and bluntly said to my aunts and my father, "I have something to tell you. Your father is dead".

'For Alison and Charlie, it meant losing a much-loved father and plummeting into a time of great turmoil and uncertainty. For Don, it meant becoming the man of the house before he was two, never having the opportunity to know his father, and growing into adolescence as a boy who must learn from his mistakes and fight his own battles, with no father to look out for him.

'My grandmother and her children lived with her parents for a few months. Then they moved into the old timber house that once stood at 18 Bentley Road, South Lismore. Grandma worked in whatever jobs she could to support the children.'

Phil was staring at Jade's thighs, where her skirt had ridden up to show the lace at the top of her stay-ups. And he was picking his nose.

Garrick pushed on: 'She took a cooking job at a Scripture Union beach mission at Kingscliff, coming up to Christmas 1960, where she met my grandfather, Humphrey Guyton, a school teacher, whom she rapidly won over with her wonderful cooking and that special charm it was that bound them together. Now that I have learned about Athol's Harley Davidson, I wonder if it might've been her appreciation of the red Vespa scooter that was Humphrey's means of transport. For the next few months, Humphrey drove that thing from Southport to Lismore every weekend, and by April 1961 they were married. After that, Grandma made him give the Vespa away, in the midst of worry about how many times he'd come off it on the highway and landed on his head!'

The packed chapel—family, Baptist Church people, latecomers standing at the back—were roaring with laughter. Garrick glanced up from his notes. Phil was edging his way closer along the pew towards Jade, now placing his snotty hand over hers. She pulled away a little, but Phil followed her.

Garrick cleared his throat. 'On teacher's wages, my grandfather took on the task of parenting three teenage children who'd been so long without a father. He was also beginning, at the age of forty-six, to father children of his own. My father asked that I acknowledge his gratitude for the efforts that Humphrey made on his behalf, and say how glad he is that Grandma chose to marry Mr Guyton, so that he could have a father to stand up to him and to encourage him to achieve at the time when he most needed that.'

Garrick watched Phil stretch his left arm up on to the back of the pew and reach to tap Jade on the shoulder. She turned in Phil's direction, looking down to where Phil was pointing with his right hand at the silver of the foil wrapped parcel that was now protruding from his hip pocket. Garrick pushed on.

'Uncle Raymond was born in December 1964. He was a precious baby with whom Grandma always retained a close and loving bond. Ray's birth came at a time of great strain for my grandmother, as earlier in her pregnancy, she had to nurse Uncle Phil back from the verge of death from all the illnesses that followed a severe burn he'd inflicted on himself by climbing up on the kitchen bench and pulling a jug of boiling water down over his arm.'

Phil was at it again. Now he was pretending to doze off, listing to the left to allow himself to bump against Jade's shoulder. He watched her body jerk at the surprise. Then she tapped Phil on the knee. They turned and exchanged a glance, then Jade giggled, looking up at Garrick, appealing. Garrick frowned back at her.

'The girls moved away to start families of their own, and Grandma had to face the terminal illness of her own mother. Great Grandma died of cancer the day before Uncle Phil's fourth birthday. Phillip told me that he thought all the visitors that came to that Anzac Day were there just for his party.

'In May the following year, the family left that house and moved into Grandma's last home in Magellan Street. My memories of Edie are tied to that house with its ramshackle garden she and Grandpa made together. I want share with you a story that Uncle Phil told me. This captures the essence of Phillip's relationship with his mother.'

Phil was still sitting too close to Jade. He sat straight, looking bright and sparky now. This part was about him.

'Phillip was five when the family moved into Magellan Street. Grandma found the house too modern. She hated the sliding doors that separated the kitchen from the lounge and dining area. She never got the knack of controlling the temperature of the hotplates on the electric range. So she put in a wood stove, with unfortunate later consequences. On the first day there, she set out to make a caramel pie, boiling up a can of condensed milk in a battered aluminium saucepan until the Nestlé label separated from the tin. The pot boiled dry. The can went bang! The neighbours registered the sound of gunfire, just as when, a few months later, her ginger beer exploded. The caramel spread to set, like fibreglass, across the ceiling. Uncle Phil climbed up on the electric stove, sanded down the lumps on the ceiling and painted over them in the summer months before he turned sixteen.'

Jade reached out her hand, placed it over Phil's and gave it a squeeze, then slowly withdrew it. Garrick watched Phil turn pink from his collar up.

'Back in 1968 my father Don was a passionate young man driving a purple iridescent EH Holden. He followed his heart and married young, with strong encouragement from my grandmother, who was determined that my place in the family should be secured. Dad and his first wife Charmaine worked hard in many jobs to sustain their family. They kept it together for seven years with my grandmother's support. Sandra's birth came four years after mine. When my mother abandoned us, Grandma stepped in to look after Sandy and me. I am very glad that my sister has flown from Dubai to be with us here today, that she was able to join me in saying goodbye to Grandma at the viewing this morning.

Jade's hand was back on Phil's again. The fat fuck looked very pleased with himself. Garrick found himself itching to meet Phil out the back after the service. Then he thought about Grandma, and pulled it together to finish the job.

'My Uncle Ray has asked me to highlight my grandmother's warmth and generosity towards anyone in need, and to tell you that she taught him to love cooking and arranging flowers, things unusually rare in a man. Dad has also asked me to mention the unexpected gift envelopes that would appear, although Grandma had so little for herself. I can also vouch for this, from my own personal experience. When I was lived in College at St Lucia, Grandma's letter would arrive with a $10 note folded inside, just when there was a textbook that I couldn't quite afford, or when the car was out of petrol with nothing but moths in my wallet.

When we put Grandpa under the ground, a few weeks after his eightieth birthday, Grandma was alone, but my Aunty Charlie and her husband Holden never left her for long. I wish to express my thanks to them, although I know that the family can never adequately repay the debt we owe them for their devotion to her care. Without their support, Grandma would never have been able to achieve what she did last Sunday, to live to a good old age in her own home, die peacefully, and cheat the nursing home out of a customer.'

Garrick, struggling to hold back tears, returned to his seat, as the congregation applauded. Phil reached out again to shake his hand. Garrick resisted the urge to give his uncle a good hard shove.

Edie's life had given rise to a long story, but more was to come. To the dismay of all present, Reverend Anderson had also prepared a sermon, themed on the reading from 2nd Corinthians, regarding 'light and momentary troubles.' This proved wearisome. Like mortal torture, eventually it came to an end.

It was almost 12.30 p.m. when the congregation rose to sing *Abide with Me*. The family trailed out behind the Szeliski boys as they wheeled the coffin to the chapel door, where the hearse waited to carry Edie Guyton to her grave. Garrick lined up in the middle on the right hand side, with Don positioned opposite him, Uncle Phil and Uncle Ray up front, and Holden and Garrick's cousin Patrick behind him. Grandma was heavy. When they lifted together, the coffin came neatly off the trolley and progressed as directed by the Szeliskis. Holden stumbled momentarily as they approached the open tailgate, but the others bore the jolt and held fast to ensure that Edie did not suffer a final indignity.

Don turned to his son, after the coffin was secured in the back of the hearse, locked in place. 'Well, one thing's for sure. Your Grandma loved her tucker. We'd better move over to shake a few hands.' They walked together around the back of the chapel to the refreshment room.

Garrick found himself across the tea cake from Günther, who had met Ray in the lobby of a concert hall in Stüttgart where he was playing flügelhorn in Lotte Schneider's orchestra. In spite of his work experience in comedy, Günther was puzzled by the day's events. 'In

Germany, funerals are very solemn occasions. But here in Australia, I come to an old lady's funeral. The grandson gives the eulogy. And everyone laughs. Again and again. All the way through. It may be that I am *Schwäbisch. Doch, alles hier its ganz unheimlich!*'

Günther was saying that, although he might be a provincial hick, everything here seemed so weird. *It must be a relief for him to exchange a few words occasionally with someone who at least has high school German*, thought Garrick. Given the distraction Jade provided, standing in her patent leather stilettoes, holding a plate of lamingtons and flirting with Reverend Anderson, he was inclined to agree with Günther. Then in the periphery of his visual field, he saw an emaciated middle-aged woman in high black boots and a red tartan miniskirt, leaning against the wall, over by the door, staring into space. Jittering, she moved her weight back and forth from one leg to the other, picked and fiddled with her skirt, clenched and unclenched her hands. Her most striking feature was her straight black hair, extending half way down her back, stark in contrast to pearlescent, slightly freckled skin. Her face was weathered and wrinkled, but no more than one might expect of an Australian woman who'd grown up in the sixties, using coconut oil to tan. What was she doing here?

'*Unheimlich? Doch, alles ist hier ganz verrückt!* Garrick responded. *Things here aren't just weird, they're quite crazy.* He excused himself and took off towards the door, just as Charmaine slipped away. Garrick looked down the drive in both directions. Then he began a frantic search behind the hedges, in the garden beds, and between the parked cars.

*

Reverend Anderson turned out to be not quite the life of the party. Jade couldn't remember the last time that she'd tried to charm a clergyman, let alone anyone wearing 'Morrie' as a moniker. 'Maurice Anderson,' he'd said, 'but you can call me Morrie!' The chances of scoring anything with Morrie were low, other than an invitation to next Saturday's Annual Sunday School Picnic. He might invite her to partner him in the three-legged race!

That fat biker seems to have a wicked streak, in spite of God's Squad and Bible College. There he is winking at me again. Standing there jiggling away, with his hands in the pockets of his leather pants. Randy old bugger. Up and down like a monkey on a trampoline. 'You'll have to excuse me, Morrie! That man over there is straining to get my attention. He looks as if he inhales another scone, he might have a heart turn. I'm a nurse you know, so I'd better attend to him.'

Jade had noticed Garrick beetling out the door, in pursuit of a junked-up grandma cougar, dressed like a streetwalker. *What's she doing here, anyway? She doesn't look like she teaches Sunday School, and she couldn't possibly be family? And why is Garrick chasing her?* Jade walked up to Phil. 'How long have you had the Ducati?' she asked. 'Any chance of a ride?'

'Well, I guess we'd better get the old lady down under, before we think about that. But if you'll come with me, I have something to show you.'

Phil walked bowlegged out the side door, with Jade following. He turned sharp left into the men's room.

Jade hesitated for a moment, looked both ways to check that no one was watching. Then she followed him in.

Phil raised his eyebrows, feigning surprise.

Jade broke into a high pitched giggle.

Phil brought his finger up to his lips to shush her. He jerked his head in the direction of an open cubicle.

It was Jade's turn to raise her eyebrows, now. Just the same, she went in.

Phil locked the cubicle door, dug deep into the right hip pocket of his leather pants, and drew out a spliff, with a twisted end, like a home-made firecracker. He put the other end in his mouth, flicked up the flame on his silver lighter, held it to the paper and drew back. He inhaled deeply, suppressing a cough as the smoke burned his throat and rushed down to fill his lungs. He held on as he passed the joint to Jade. She popped the wet end into her mouth and sucked.

Jade spluttered.

Phil doubled up, wheezing out his laugh. Smoke gushed out of his nose as though from the the rear end of a Mazda 1200 that had done its rings. Fortunately someone in the next cubicle flushed, masking the sound. Phil leaned into Jade, who'd brought the joint up to her mouth and was about to suck in again, placed his mouth over the smouldering end and blew. Puff rushed all the way down her bronchial tree. Phil took the joint from her mouth and drew back on it again, pulled it out, pursed his lips, tilted his head up and puffed three little smoke rings over the top of the white-glossed melamine partition. Then he leant towards her face and puckered up his lips.

Jade pushed him in the belly, turned her head away and squeaked, 'Hey, you're getting a bit fresh!'

Phil was confused. He shrugged, dumped the squib of the joint in the bowl, and flushed. *Another Saturday night's fun and games down the gurgler.* He unlocked the cubicle, poked his head out to check that all was clear, then traipsed out through the washroom and into the open air.

Jade followed, colliding with Garrick, who was pacing up and down outside, wide-eyed and frantic.

'That's one hell of a girl you've got there!' quipped Phil.

'Shut the fuck up, or I'll shove your Bible so far up your arse that you choke on Deuteronomy!'

*

It was a ten minute drive, via Oliver Avenue and Skyline Road, to the Lismore Cemetery. 'What do you think I imagined you were doing with Phil in the toilets?' snapped Garrick at the wheel of the Beemer.

'And what were you doing chasing that slag?' retorted Jade.

'That slag,' screamed Garrick, braking suddenly, 'is my mother!' The black sedan skidded on the gravel before coming to a stop, just a few feet from the back of the hearse, near where Holden was staring down, seemingly mesmerised by his size eleven feet. The Szeliski boys were pacing anxiously. Garrick slammed the driver's door and walked over to take up his position with the other pall bearers, mumbling apologies.

'Where's Phil? asked Don.

'I don't know, Dad!'

'Well, he'd better get here quick. That Scotsman's being paid by the minute.' Don nodded in the direction of the piper in Maclean o' Duart tartan standing by the open grave, under the jacaranda, chanters squealing as he pushed on the bellows.

Just then the Ducati roared through the cemetery gates and up the drive. Phil almost spun a 360 on that spot that Garrick'd hit a couple of minutes earlier. He kicked the stand into place, pulled off his helmet and sauntered over.

'Take your time, brother,' muttered Don.

'You don't look well,' said Ray.

'When you're ready, gentlemen,' prompted Pete Szeliski.

The piper squeezed the bellows and launched into the first bars of *Amazing Grace*. Six men bent their knees, and on a signal from Pete, they lifted. Slowly they began their progress forward.

Most of the family had come to the graveside. All the hangers on from the church had been sent on their way, but that still left forty or so sons, daughters, grandsons, nieces, nephews, their spouses and offspring, all waiting to pay their last respects to Edie Guyton. Her sister Jeanie and her brother Doug had been thought too frail to stand. By now they would be ready for another cup of tea, waiting at the old Guyton home, for when things at the cemetery were over. Athol Willis's grave was nearby, and so was Ron Ormiston's. Grandpa Guyton waited down below. The gravediggers had been discreet enough not to quite uncover his box.

The casket was brought to rest on the chrome frame. A wreath of lilies, roses and white gladioli lay on top. None of the pall bearers fell into the grave. Morrie Anderson stepped forward. 'Dear friends, the time has come for us to commit the soul of our much loved Edith to her Lord Jesus, who has welcomed her into his arms, and to lay her body to rest in the ground.' The Szeliskis released the pinions. The pulleys began to lower the box down into the hole. Stan Szeliski held out a bag, from which Morrie took a scoop of sand and poured it down on to the coffin, saying: 'Earth to earth, ashes to ashes, dust to dust. Just as the Lord God has breathed life into this shell, in His own time, in accordance with His will, He has taken life away. I now invite each of you to come forward to say goodbye to Edie in your own way. You may choose to place flowers, or precious objects, or to take a scoop of sand from Stan and scatter it in the grave.'

Alison went first, with her son Patrick to support her. Then came Charlie and Holden, Don and Christine, Phil and Ray. Günther hung back at a discreet distance, leaning against the jacaranda. Garrick stepped forward, with Sandy on one side and Jade on the other. He disengaged his right arm from Jade's elbow and dipped into the left breast pocket of his suit, pulled out a macadamia shell, and tossed it in. A thunk rose out of the grave as the object bounced off the coffin.

'What was that?' whispered Jade.

'Grandma was born in Kingaroy. She planted that tree from a seedling raised on her parents' farm—a Queensland nut!'

NOT COMING TO THE WEDDING

There was little opportunity for Garrick to speak with Jade after the funeral. Sandy was in the back seat as they drove back to Goonellabah. Jade packed her things that morning and left for Brisbane immediately after the burial, ready for a four day stint of night shifts starting that evening.

Don poured Garrick a glass of Shiraz. 'You did a great job of telling your Grandma's story today, Garrick. But there's something I have to say to you. We're a very open and welcoming family. I hate to think of anyone taking the piss out of us, least of all out of you. Things I've noticed make me think that girl of yours would make a better mistress than a wife. I hope you're not planning to marry her, because if you are, I'm not coming to the wedding.'

Garrick almost choked on a lump of roast. Don was not usually this frank with him. He'd said almost nothing when Garrick was in the midst of the troubles with Penny. And things were difficult enough. He wanted to ask his Dad if he had noticed Charmaine, if he had any sense of what she might've been doing there, or of why she had taken off so suddenly. But that would stir up more trouble. Charmaine wasn't someone who could be talked about in this house. There was too much pain around her. But he needed confirmation of the sighting. If it wasn't that Jade had seen her too, he would still be wondering if she had been a ghost.

Garrick took a big gulp of the wine his father had poured. It burned at the back of his throat, long after he swallowed. 'There are times, you know, Dad, when I wish my Grandpa was still alive. Times when I wish I could talk to him again. Sorry, Christine, the food's great, but I think I'll go for a drive.'

It wasn't like Garrick to pass on lamb. He got up from the table, picked up his keys and walked out into the crisp August evening. He drove down to Kadina Park, where his grandfather took him to play when Don was away at the mines. He got out of the car and sat down on a park bench near the barbecues, just out of the direct range of the overhead lights. A couple of teenage girls were playing on the roundabout across the path, still in their Lismore High School uniforms. Their socks hung loose around their ankles. They had unbuttoned their white blouses and tied them in knots at the front to reveal their slender bellies. Their black-and-white checked pleated skirts were hitched up high and folded down at the waist. 'Hey mister,' called the girl with her hair in long dark plaits, 'you got a cigarette?'

Garrick smiled and shrugged.

'Just one cigarette?' she pleaded.

'Sorry, don't smoke!' Garrick shouted back.

'You got any money?'

That was the kind of trouble Garrick didn't need. He got up and walked back to the BMW, activated the ignition and drove around aimlessly for about half an hour before heading back home.

*

He slept fitfully that night. Dreams came in fragments, scenes in which he was chasing after impossible women, women who always seemed further away, no matter how close he was to catching them.

Charmaine stood in a clearing, dressed in her black boots and tartan mini, looked over her shoulder and beckoned to him, then turned and walked into the forest. He ran after her, but she blended into the trees. From every one of them her voice rang out, mocking him. 'Gar-rick! Gar-rick!'

Then somehow it was Jade and Rachel, as naughty schoolgirls, soliciting outside the Night Owl on Main Street in Woolloongabba, near the Pineapple Hotel. Jade's hair was punked up short and spikey, Rachel's long, black and sleek. Just as he was about to cross at the lights when that Myshkin fellow walked up to them, drew a wad of cash out the pocket of his Levi 511s, took one girl on each arm and walked away with them. They both turned back to laugh as he stood waiting for the lights to change.

Garrick tried to sleep, but couldn't shut down the cinema of cruel Lolitas running in his head, nor stave off the flood of images of violent retaliation, of the wounds inflicted on the bodies of each hapless coquette. He sat up, swung his feet over the side of the bed, pulled on his blue flannel robe, slipped into his ugg boots and padded out to sit at the kitchen table with his pen, his notebook and a tattered Penguin paperback edition of *The Idiot*.

Writing might help, but Garrick found himself in such a state of agitation that putting pen to paper was impossible.

RETURN OF THE EVIL YOUTH FOR CHRIST

Nick found it worked better to go into gigs at the Zoo fully loaded. So there he was, an hour before opening time, outside the entrance on Ann Street, staring at his own poster as if it was an alien life form worthy of his best efforts at engaging conversation. If ever intergalactic diplomacy failed and the squid-like life-forms spurned the friendly hand extended, Nick would be there with his black Fender 70s Jazz Bass in its hard case, ready to burst back into the action as soon as the aliens reversed the shrink ray. The poster read:

Return of the Evil Youth for Christ
play the Zoo
launch new EP Necronomicon
Saturday 31st August
Plus Spoken Word Open Mic Haiku Slam
Doors: 8.00 p.m.
$30 Student Concession $20
Upstairs 711 Ann Street Fortitude Valley

As the poster was not talking back, and no door bitch responded to his knock, Nick picked up his back pack and his bass and walked up the street, down the lane and round the back where the rest of the band were unloading amps and the drum kit from Ned's XR6 Ford Falcon ute.

'Hey Nick! Where are those girls you keep crapping on about? Weren't you supposed to be bringing the pussy tonight?'

'Fuck up and die, Ned!' Nick gave his mate a stiff-arm shove in the chest.

Ned bounced against the brickwork with all the puff knocked out of him. 'Whoa man! Easy! You're all strung, just a little too tight. I hope you've saved some pills for us—something better than your Epilim? There's gotta be something to supplement the couple of jugs of beer Wah-wah's old man, that stingy bastard, expects us to share with the whole band? You got some eccys? Or are you saving them up for toolie time at schoolies? Get your bass upstairs and come and help me shift these drums.'

Nick'd had so many pills he was rattling. And a couple of points of crystal meth. The beer drought was not likely to be too much of a worry for him. As for Ned, Geoff, Dave, Mike and any girls they might pick up, they knew he could fix them quick for a fifty, and his backpack was stuffed tight with tabs.

With the drums, the mikes and the amps in place, and all the cords secured with duct tape, it was time fur tuning up and checking the sound. Dave was down there on the mixer, signalling to Geoff to rattle something up on the drums. Nick joined in with a bass riff. Dave dropped the volume on the woofers and upped the reverb on the mikes. The crowd were drifting in. Pretty thin, but what could you expect at this time of the night?

Down there at the bar, Jade and Rachel were waving at him, calling out 'Nick!'

It's that blonde nurse, and her chink mate from Canada. And who's that they've got in tow? Shit a brick! It's the Doc! Nick touched Ned on the shoulder and said to him, 'Look yonder, oh ye of little faith! The pussy's just arrived.'

Ned grinned and punched him in the belly, pulling at the last moment.

*

In the queue to pass security, Garrick felt uncomfortable. His black pants, blue-and-white striped shirt, sports jacket and side-zippered Doc Martens boots made him seem conservatively overdressed in the midst of the grungy twenty-somethings in their checked shirts, skinny jeans, Connies and train driver caps. Most of the girls wore minis and stilettoes, but there were a few in boots and jeggings. Skulls and roses seemed to be the most popular motif. Garrick was in the queue just behind a tall redhead in a Hell Bunny dress. There were so many tattoos. Jade and Rachel were just behind him, waving their complementary passes about, preening and fluttering their eyelashes. He thought the girls blended better than he did. As he was with them, hopefully they'd let him in.

Garrick looked back across the road and up at the hoarding on the side of the building opposite. It used to be the Brisbane City Mission, founded in 1859 and administered during the Great Depression by The Good Samaritan of Fortitude Valley, the clergyman who'd married Grandpa Guyton's sister, Great Aunty June. He'd recently found a video of her on YouTube, distributing blankets to the poor in 1939. The sign on the side of the building facing up Ann Street used to say: 'Jesus Died for Your Sins!'

Now here was Garrick, queuing for a ticket to see Return of the Evil Youth for Christ. How the girls had come by complimentaries was a

102

mystery, one he considered beneath his dignity to question. Jade had declared that she and Rachel were going. If he didn't want to spend Saturday evening alone, he'd be coming too. There would be poetry, she said. She'd expect him to get up and do something for the open mic, although he couldn't imagine any form of barbarism exceeding that of a haiku slam.

The security guy's biceps were popping with veins like branch lines on a metropolitan rail network as they bulged out of his short-sleeved muscle shirt. He gave Garrick a wink as he looked the girls up and down, then motioned them towards the woman at the door. She was wearing silver stiletto sandals, an 'I Heart Zombies' t-shirt, stretch polyester-and-spandex skirt and black fishnets. Her blonde hair hung straight at the back to below her waist. She had more kohl around her eyes than Morticia Addams channelling a Turkish belly dancer. She smiled as she took Garrick's money, scanned the girls' passes, stamped their wrists and sent them up the stairs.

The bar was up the back, to the left of the entrance at the top of the stairs. There were a few metal chairs scattered around tables at that end of the space up front near the dance floor—polished hardwood, worn in places, and neither slippery nor shiny. The musicians were warming up. Garrick went to the bar and ordered himself a Crown Lager and lime Vodka Cruisers for the girls.

Jade began waving her arms and shouting 'Nick!'.

Garrick turned to see what all the fuss was about. Rachel was smiling and waving too. The base player was waving back. It was that drug-dealing epileptic patient of his, Nick Myshkin.

*

103

The band opened with *Black Betty*, Nick Myshkin on backing vocals. When they followed up with a cover of Hole's *Malibu*, Nick pulled on a blonde wig and a pair of man-sized heels to sing the lead in place of Courtney Love. The crowd went wild. The band segued into David Bowie's *Sorrow*, Ned singing lead, with Nick hamming it up on all the lines about 'long blonde hair'.

When the band moved into their own material, the launch of the ominously named *Necronomicon* EP, Jade seemed to lost in the single note thrumming of the bass beat and the drone of the singers' growling out something that might've registered on sonar as the noise a giant squid makes when it's in its death throws. 'Cthulhu, cthulhu ...' Maybe being lost was what it was all about, and if Jade`` was lost, then so were most of the crowd, who seemed to Garrick, with himself the exception, to be having fun and enjoying the evening.

After the EP launch, the band took a break, which Ned announced would be followed by the haiku slam. All intending participants were to register with Dave, who would also judge the slam, with the prize going to the poet who elicited the loudest audience response.

While Garrick registered, Nick strode over to the table, hugged both the girls enthusiastically, slipped them each a pill, and offered to buy them drinks. He was away at the bar when Garrick returned. Nick came up with a tray of Vodka Cruisers, said 'Hi Doc, sorry I didn't have any idea what you were drinking! Enjoying the show?'

'I see you've got a talent for the bass!' replied Garrick.

Then Ned began announcing the contestants. Seven brave souls had entered, with Garrick sixth on the list. When Garrick was called to the microphone, he offered this:

> *September night*
> *too chill for the moon*
> *stars plunge into the pool*

There was muted applause. Jade noticed Rachel was clapping, so she clapped too. Then Garrick hung around the mike too long, as if expecting something more.

He's a bit of a dickhead, really. Acts as if it all should be high art. Then he's pissed off when they don't get it, she thought.

Nick was the last contestant to be called. He walked up to the mike, took it from the stand and spat out:

> *Charley Bukowski*
> *nearly had an erection.*
> *Quick! More alcohol!*

The crowd roared and hooted and clapped so loudly that Dave's decibel meter knocked over the top of the scale. Nick was the clear winner! He bowed and smiled and blew kisses in all directions. Ned jumped up beside him, awarded him the prize and then announced him as the featured spoken word artist for the evening.

Nick went over to where he'd racked his bass, picked up his blonde wig, slipped on his pumps, hung a syringe on a piece of string as a necklace, smeared his lips with a tube of cherry lipstick, and tottered back to the microphone to announce:

For my loss, this sadness never ends.
Ask any widow, black the hole
blocked off with spider's web
behind the veil. With this syringe
I stop my breath. Only your kiss
(I'm growing pale) can bring me back
from DEATH!

Nick leapt from the stage and ran, arms flailing, over to the table where Garrick sat with the girls. He grabbed Garrick by the front of his shirt, lifted him up and leaned in to clinch a kiss. Both men fell forward, over Garrick's chair. Nick landed on top, slobbering and smearing all over Garrick's face. Garrick spluttered and pushed at Nick, thrusting him away. Nick broke into a high-pitched laugh as Garrick struggled to his feet with cherry lips all over his face. He ran for the door as Nick pursued, high heels clack-clack-clacking on the hardwood floor. Garrick tumbled down the stairs, picked himself up and ran out into the street before Nick turned, still laughing and bounded back up the stairway, poked his head through the entrance and roared, 'Who's next?' The crowd erupted into raucous laughter.

*

Garrick's heart was racing. He staggered up Ann Street towards Kemp Place and the Story Bridge. When he collided with a couple outside Cloudland, he received a shove into the traffic and 'Watch where you're going, mate!' He was given cause to thank the ABS breaking system on the Black-and-White taxi that would otherwise have cleaned him up. He struggled round the corner and negotiated several more crossings before he realised where he was, on the outbound pedestrian walkway of the Story Bridge, making his way painfully towards Kangaroo Point. He looked down at the muddy waters of the Brisbane River below and momentarily considered throwing himself off, then collected his wits and walked on. The Angel Moroni on the skyline saluted him with his rampant trumpet as he approached the Pineapple Hotel, where he managed to flag another taxi down. He scarcely noticed the lonely figure patrolling the other side of the road. The taxi took him home to Dornoch Terrace, where he collapsed, fully clothed, into his bed.

In the dream, Garrick walked across the bridge, his body numb with despair. Each step was like lifting an elephant in a lead-lined coffin. Everything was enveloped in thick fog. As his hand clutched the railing, he found it wet with cold condensation. Suddenly, his eyes were blinded by a torch beam. He blinked. As his pupils accommodated, he began to make out the figure barring his way— that of a tall pale woman with flaming red hair hanging down in curls on either side of the peak of a police cap with a black-and-white chequered band. She wore motorcycle boots with gaiters and tight black leathers. She held the torch in her left hand, shining insistently into his eyes. Her face was whited with zinc, to a geisha effect. Her lips were blood red, like those of the late Marcel Marceau. She raised her right hand, commanding him to stop. Her black cycle gloves dripped fresh blood, running from puncture wounds in the cubital veins inside the elbows on both arms.

'Turn around, Garrick Willis,' she commanded in a brown voice, more like that to be expected from Louis Armstrong or Paul Robeson. 'Your friends are in danger, and you must go to them!'

Her eyes rolled back into her head, showing the whites. Then the lids fell over them. Her face turned blue. She fell, and as he screamed, the torch dropped and went out. She dissolved into the mist.

He woke to the beat of his pounding heart, to himself in the empty room, in the lonely bed, to his pillow slip smeared with cherry lipstick.

*

The next thing Jade knew, she was naked in her bed in the cottage at the Wellington Road end of Toohey Street, her sheets wet with blood from puncture wounds inside both elbows and trickling from below the clotted mass of hair over her pubic mound. She was about to scream when she heard a banging sound coming from Grandma's bedroom. She grabbed the iron crow bar that she kept by the bed and ran across the corridor. She swung the door open. Ned was clutching Rachel's body by the hips, fucking her hard, doggy-style. The banging was her head making contact, like a coconut, with the bed head, with each thrust. Rachel was like a rag doll, unconscious, froth and vomit dribbling out of the corner of her mouth.

'Stop!' screamed Jade, raising the iron bar, ready to brain Ned right across his shaven pate.

Ned took a look around, pulled out, grabbed his shirt and jeans, pushed past her as she swung at him and missed. He ran down the hall, out the door, across the verandah and out into the street.

Jade jumped on the bed, hauled Rachel onto her left side, stuck her fingers into her mouth and scooped around the back of her throat, hauling out a bolus of vomit, mucus, cum and congealed blood. Rachel coughed, gasped and heaved, belching forth more of the soup. Jade cleared the airway again, satisfied herself that Rachel's breasts were moving up and down as her rib cage expanded and contracted, and that her lips had already turned from deathly blue to a bruised shade of red. She pulled the doona up over the naked body of her friend, then grabbed an old dressing gown from Grandma's wardrobe, wrapped it around herself, picked up the iron bar and systematically searched the house, lining herself up on the wall with the weapon raised before poking her head around each corner and each doorway to ensure that the room was clear, that Nick and the other boys had also gone. Then she ran for the phone and called 000.

'Fire, police or ambulance?'

'Get an ambulance, please, quick!'

'Connecting you now.'

Jade realised she shouldn't have left Rachel, so she rushed back to her as the ambulance triage operator took her details. Fortunately she was still breathing, but hadn't yet come round.

About five minutes later, the ambulance and the paramedic arrived in separate vehicles, almost simultaneously, sirens wailing down the little street. After a quick assessment, they had Rachel under the sheets and the space blanket, onto a gurney and into the back of the van.

'Can you please take us to the Mater?' Jade pleaded. 'We both work at Princess Alexandra Hospital. We know everyone there in emergency.'

Jade climbed in and took a seat beside Rachel, who was still unconscious. As the van turned the corner into Main Street and sped towards the Stanley Street corner, Jade peered out the window and caught a glimpse of an emaciated middle-aged woman in high black boots and red tartan miniskirt, her long black hair falling all the way down her back as she paced up and down the footpath from the Night Owl to the Southern Cross Motel.

FATHER'S DAY

Garrick tried to persuade the women to report the violence to the police. The staff at the Mater called in the sexual assault worker as soon as they had checked out Rachel and found that Jade's cardiorespiratory status was stable. After a shot of Narcan, Rachel regained consciousness, just before the sexual assault specialist arrived. Both refused to allow the examination, and neither was willing to make a statement. They also refused to give blood samples for toxicology, but later realised they'd better let some blood be sent to test for hepatitis B, hepatitis C, and HIV. They also allowed the doctor to take swabs for chlamydia and other STDs, to collect urine samples for microscopy and culture, and to examine them for vaginal tears which, thankfully, proved minor, not requiring surgical repair. It was too early for pregnancy tests, but the doctor insisted they do them anyway. Rachel was required to stay in overnight, but after Jade received a shot of intravenous antibiotics to cover her for syphilis and gonorrhoea, she called up Garrick to collect her.

By then it was 4.30 Sunday morning, Father's Day. All over the city, whole families of health fanatics were waking and dressing in running gear, making their way by car, bus or train to the Murarrie end of the Gateway Bridge, to line up in their tens of thousands for the Bridge to Brisbane Fun Run. Garrick had planned to give it a miss this year. Just as well, given the previous night's misadventure.

Garrick lay on the right hand side of the bed, with Jade clutching onto him for comfort. He looked down at her, covered in bruises, and with needle tracks up and down her arms. The dragonfly had been torn off her belly button stud. And were those cigarette burns?

Sleep was impossible. Whenever he closed his eyes, Nick's leering face with red lips and the blonde wig came to him. His nostrils filled with the rank smell of the man's body odour, and the sour taste of his mouth, accompanied by the urge to gag and retch.

But it was Father's Day, and soon he would need to rise, shower, dress and drive over to Ascot to collect his son. Tom was to spend the day with him and be returned to his mother before dinner. Garrick had planned to take him with Jade on a paddle-wheeler cruise up the river to the Lone Pine sanctuary. He had promised to show Tom the animals. He looked at Jade again and thought that it might be better if Tom did not see her like this. But why should he be feeling so ashamed? It wasn't damage that he had done.

The clock was showing seven. Jade continued to sleep, occasionally snoring. Garrick slipped out of bed, padded softly to the shower, immersed himself, towelled, and pulled on his jeans and a fresh t-shirt. He made his way to the kitchen, grabbed his car keys, slipped on his sandals by the door, and headed out.

*

When Garrick arrived, Tom had not yet had breakfast. Penny was cold and officious, but had helped Tom select a card. She had written in it for him, and bought and wrapped a box of Darrell Lea chocolates. 'Well, you are his father, after all,' said Penny, when Garrick thanked her, commenting that he had not been expecting this.

'Are you going to share them with me, Dad?' asked Tom

'Sure, Tom, after we get you some breakfast. What would you like?'

'Can we go to McDonald's?'

As they came up to the drive-thru, Garrick asked Tom what he wanted.

'Hot cakes, Dad!'

Garrick ordered three serves, drove further up to the window to receive them, and then on to Highgate Hill.

'Is Aunty Jade coming with us to Lone Pine, Dad?'

'She's still sleeping. I think she might be too tired. She had a bad headache last night. We'll see how she feels after she's had coffee and some breakfast.'

'Is coffee good for headaches, Dad?'

'Sometimes, Tom! Sometimes.'

*

Is it the Dunwich Horror? Jade did not like what she saw in the mirror. The bruises were beginning to come out around her cheekbones. Her head was throbbing. She took a couple of Nurofen from the canister on the ledge above the basin and swallowed them. There was a small haemorrhage under the outer layer of the white of her right eye. It was beginning to occur to her that she had been lucky to come out of this alive. She would call in sick for work. There was no way that she could turn up there like this. So far she'd been able to hide evidence of her recent habits. *I'm not going to let it all slip now. I need my job.* She found a tube of Hirudoid cream in the drawer in the vanity basin and began to rub it into the bruises. Then she sat down to pee. It stung like buggery.

By now, the craving was beginning to set in again. She fiddled with her hair and picked at the quicks of her fingernails. Soon Garrick'd be back with Tom, who'd be all over her and into everything. That was enough to bring on the sensation of insects crawling under her skin, without the withdrawal symptoms.

Jade heard the key turning in the front door lock. Surprising how sharp her senses were. And even more, how much it startled her.

'Are you there, Jade?' enquired Garrick, through the bathroom door.

'Hello, Aunty Jade! We've got hot cakes!'

'Hello, Tom! I'll be out in a minute. Garrick, would you put some coffee on?'

Jade picked up her white cotton towelling robe and wrapped it around herself after spraying her chest with *Ysatis*. She squeezed toothpaste onto a brush and cleaned her teeth. She spat a lot of blood when she rinsed.

'Hurry up, Aunty Jade! Your hotcakes are getting cold.'

*

They had a seafood buffet lunch on board the *Mirimar* on the way to Lone Pine. The prawns were neither as large nor as fresh as they should be. That didn't stop Jade from taking her plate around three times, with a quick trip to the toilet in between helpings.

On the trip back from Fig Tree Pocket, Garrick pulled out the framed polaroid shot he'd purchased of the two of them standing behind Tom, while the little man cuddled a sedated koala. 'Don't we make a lovely family!' he quipped.

They walked to the BMW from the peer. Garrick drove Tom home to Ascot. Jade waited across the road in the parked car during the handover.

'Do you think he had a good day?' asked Garrick, pulling out from the curb to head back to Highgate Hill.

'He seemed happy enough.'

'I think he really likes you.'

'That's all very well, but I don't think you'll ever want to be a father to my baby.'

This was about all that Garrick needed just now. 'Let's talk about that some more when we get home.'

They finished the journey in silence. Once they were back at the unit, Garrick reached out for her and pulled her to him, gently and tenderly. 'So you want to talk about having a baby?'

'Well, not just now. I think I'm going to be too sore to fuck for at least a week!'

'But is that what you're wanting?

'I don't know. I can't see that I'd be able to rely on you. You're not even divorced. And I think you'll go back to her soon anyway. You're always talking about how you should be with her.'

'That's ridiculous! Come here!' Garrick reached to draw Jade closer, intending to kiss her. She pulled away and fled into the bedroom, locking the door behind her. Soon he could hear her sobbing. 'Hey, don't do that, honey! Let me in! Let's talk some more about it.'

After a minute or so, Jade opened the door a crack and peaked around it. There were tears rolling down her cheeks, but she was already quite naked. Garrick found himself intensely aroused. 'All right,' she said, 'but get your clothes off, and come in here.'

As he lay down beside her, Garrick noticed that she was breaking out in gooseflesh all over her thighs, and there was cold sweat on her arms and on her forehead. 'How long have you been mainlining?' he asked.

She turned on him suddenly, with a vicious snarl. 'Why do you ask that?'

'Darling, I'm a doctor. I can tell that you are going into narcotic withdrawal. You had a lot of shit stuck in you last night, but you wouldn't be breaking out like this if that was the only time. I've wondered before when I've seen you with those band-aids inside your elbow and on the backs of your hands.'

'Leave me alone!' yelled Jade. She pulled the sheet over her head and slid down the bed.

'I'd thought maybe you'd been popping crystal meth, but you're looking more like it's heroin now. And you seemed to know that fellow Nick too well. You realise he's my patient, don't you?'

'Holy fuck! How dare you accusee me! You smartarse, with your puny little prick! All you do is carry on with sexual demands, expecting me to be there all the time to make you feel good. I'm not sure whether I'm there to babysit you, or your horrible kid. You just want to take it all, and never give. And if I had a baby with you, you'd be chasing after some other skirt while I was still in the hospital, probably trying to get a leg over the midwife just as its head was popping out. I could never trust you to be a father to my kid. You're a miserable worm and you just don't give a shit. Why don't you just fuck up and die!'

'Get out!' he screamed at her, raising his hand and slapping her hard across the face. His hand moved ever so slowly and he heard the crack as if it was coming from far away. 'Get out, bitch!' he screamed again.

Jade reached up to touch herself on the cheek where it was stinging. She felt strangely alive, like a hunted animal. She sprung off the bed, grabbed her gown and ran, screaming, 'Fuck!'

Garrick heard the front door of the unit slam.

A LETTER TO MY LOVE

A late cancellation in clinic gave Garrick an opportunity to draft a letter to Nick Myshkin.

Dear Mr Myshkin

Due to your unfortunately aggressive behaviour towards me when we met by chance at a social event last Saturday evening, I am not able to continue as your treating neurologist. I will write to your referring doctor, Christine Smythe, to summarise my findings and treatment plan. You should consult Dr Smythe, who will be able to advise you as to the adequacy or otherwise of your current Epilim dose of 400mg twice daily, provided that you have attended Queensland Medical Laboratories for your blood test as previously advised. Should the need arise again for you to consult a neurologist, I will not be able to make myself available to you for consultation In that event, you should consult Dr Smythe and seek a referral to another neurologist.

Yours sincerely

Dr Garrick Willis   cc Dr Christine Smythe

Garrick printed three copies on his letterhead, signed them, addressed an envelope to Nick, and gave it to the receptionist to put in the post. He quickly penned another letter to Christine, outlining the clinical findings, diagnosis and recommended treatment, with an added line saying that he would be happy to discuss the reasons for his decision to cease treating Myshkin, should she wish to call him. He enveloped Christine's letter, together with her copy of the one to Nick. Hopefully that would be the last he would see of that man.

But would Jade stay away from him? It seemed she may have already had too much of a taste, and that she was spiralling downwards. Garrick worried about her, but it was over between them.

Jade returned to the unit briefly to collect her things while Garrick was at work. She left a note in an envelope, together with her key, saying that he should not expect to hear from her again, and not to show his face around at Toohey Street. He didn't. But he called her mobile several times. She did not answer or respond to the messages he left.

How was Rachel? On Monday, Garrick dropped in at the Mater at lunch time, brought her flowers. She seemed pleased to see him. He thought she was doing okay, but he could see the shine had been knocked off her confidence. She was not likely to be ebullient any time soon. They sent her home that afternoon, after a CT brain scan. She asked Garrick to meet her for a drink on Friday at the Chalk Hotel after work. He reluctantly admitted to himself that he was looking forward to seeing her, not just because she might have word from Jade.

*

Jade grabbed her keys, her phone and her purse from the kitchen as she headed out the door from Garrick's unit. She walked to the top of Highgate Hill and turned left into Hampstead Road, where she managed to flag down a taxi.

Jade leaned against the left passenger door and let out a huge yawn as the cab turned into Vulture Street, heading towards the 'Gabba.

'That was a big one,' remarked the driver. 'Since you're already in your nightie, I'm wondering if you need a place to sleep?'

'Just take me where I told you. My girlfriend's waiting for me. She's a cop, and I called her just before I flagged you down. She knows I'm coming home in a taxi. If she doesn't see me home within half an hour, she'll be out after me. You want me to call her now?'

'Jesus, lady! I was just trying to help.'

By the time the taxi arrived at Toohey Street, Jade was sweating profusely, her eyes and nose were watering, and she was beginning to experience terrible cramps in her belly.

The driver noticed that her hands were shaking as she passed him her credit card. 'You sure you're all right, lady?' he asked.

'Fine. Thanks for asking!' she snapped back at him. By now the gooseflesh had spread upwards from her legs and was erupting all over her body. She wanted to get out of the cab and up the stairs before she hurled, and especially before she lost control of her bowels. She got through the gate, belching and retching, then threw up all over the stairs. She unlocked the front door and raced to the bathroom, where she vomited twice more into the toilet, then sat down and fouled the bowl with the product of gut-wrenching spasms of her colon.

Jade didn't feel safe anymore in the house, not after what had gone down last night. She couldn't quite tell whether the noises she heard were inside or outside, and it was hard to hear at all above the sound of her own chattering teeth. Every shadow was that of a hostile intruder. And the last person she wanted to see was Nick, but she just had to get a hit, and get it quick. She reached in her pocket for her phone.

Nick answered. 'Hello? Had a nice time last night?'

'You're an arsehole!' Jade screamed into the phone, then remembered that he was an arsehole that she needed, just as hers exploded again and squirted all over the white ceramic.

'I like it when you're angry!' Nick said. 'What can I do for you?'

'I need a hit, Nick! I'm withdrawing. I had no idea that it could be like this.'

'Ice or smack?'

'Both, but more smack. And quick!'

'Slow down, little lady. I'm busy here on a job at the moment, down at the Southern Cross Motel. And you're going to have to do something for Daddy, if you want Daddy to bring you sugar ...'

'I just need it so badly, Nick. Please, Nick! Don't be such an arsehole. Get over here and help! You're only just down the road.'

'But it's not so simple, little baby It's not all about you. If you want sugar, you're going to have to do a job for Daddy.'

'What?' She was already nauseous, and very soon she would be overwhelmed by her own stench. She had to stop shitting, or the vomiting would start again. Her bowels rumbled and she trumpeted out a noxious fart that could have been the pride of a military bugler.

'When you talk so sweetly to your Daddy, you get him hard and drive him so wild that he can hardly think. Now what was it that I was wanting you to do? Oh yes, there's a boarding house on the corner of Harcourt and Brunswick Streets in New Farm, just up from the Valley.

Go over there and wait for Daddy in room 6. You'll find that the main door is unlocked, and the key to room 6 is under the mat.'

'Why don't you just finish up what you're doing at the Southern Cross and come down the street? I'll do whatever you want, but here, and quick!'

'Patience, child! Patience and obedience. If baby girl wants sweet things, then she will do what needs to be done to please her Daddy. So get over there! And when Daddy comes home, he will show you what he needs you to do.' Nick hung up the call.

*

Garrick snuck away from work for a haircut at lunch time on Friday. He took the BMW out of the hospital car park, turned into Ipswich Road, to the Gabba corner, where he turned towards West End, eventually parking behind Calliope's Salon, next door to Thanh Le's Restaurant in Hardgrave Road.

Calliope Piakis rushed up to him immediately, her wide hips swaying, her long black hair curling down over her shoulders. 'Dr Willis! So good to see you again! Can I get you a coffee while Spiro washes your hair?'

'Sure Cally! Flat white would be great. Please just call me Garrick.' He fumbled in his pocket and brought out the folded A4 sheet. 'I have this poem I wrote after the last time I was here. I wanted to show you.'

'A poem, for me!' Cally squealed and fluttered the long black lashes over her blue-green eyes. She was excited. Ever since Demetrios left her, she had been looking at Garrick as a potential catch. She always booked him on to her personal list.

'Well, not exactly,' said Garrick.

Cally deflated, but she took the poem from him anyway, her thin pencilled eyebrows furrowed, her lips pursed into a pout. 'I'll read it while Spiro does his thing, then I'll be back with you in a minute, darling.' She turned away. 'Spiro,' she called, 'make Dr Willis a flat white, and then wash him up at basin 1!' She took the poem out the back and carefully unfolded it.

Hair Care Products

At the hairdresser
Leanne gets me coffee
and a questionnaire.

I tick the 'rarely' box
for the question about how often
people offer
compliments about my hair.

She cuts it like I ask her.
The shorter the better
now I'm going balder.

She wants to sell me
masculine shampoo
repair conditioner
hair restorer.

Leanne can tell
that I'm a tough customer.

She asks if I believe in UFOs
while she cuts away
at the back of my neck
with a cut throat razor.

I tell her that the aliens
have used my bald patch
as a launch pad
for their spacecraft.

Leanne tells me
that she had a bald patch
but she rubbed it daily
with the hair restorer.

She tells me women
have been known
to use the masculine shampoo.

Her arms wave wildly
with the cut throat razor.
I reach for my wallet.
I leave with several
hair care products.

When she returned there was a little tear welled up in the corner of Calliope's left eye. She dabbed at it with a tissue, careful not to smudge her mascara, then faced her persecutor, dismissing Spiro abruptly to broom duty. 'I let Leanne go last week,' she said. 'What can I do for you today, honey? Will you let me black your sideburns, get rid of all that nasty grey?'

Garrick realised that he had hurt her feelings. He'd been trying to give her a hint about Leanne and Spiro, and the need for her to send them for customer sensitivity training. 'No thanks, Cally, don't make me like a Greek boy. But it is time for a change. I'd like you to take it all off with the clippers, with no blade, then do the back of my neck with the razor.'

'All right, honey, but you would look so good with it all dyed black. Make you look five years younger!'

*

The cab brought Jade to the corner of Brunswick and Harcourt Streets. She paid the driver and stepped out with the carry-on bag in which she kept toiletries, a work uniform, a fresh towel, and a change of clothes. She was shaking so much that she struggled to unlatch the gate of 548 Brunswick Street. She pulled her bag up to the front door under the portico of the large two storey house with the sign announcing 'HARCOURT LODGE—Casual and Permanent Rental—Low Rates—Vacancy'. Jade glanced across the road, meeting the gaze of a tall redheaded woman in black leathers and motorcycle boots who was leaning against the wall beside the door of the Laundromat, puffing on a cigarette.

The main door of the house was unlocked, just as Nick had said it would be. The hallway was poorly lit. A termite infested hardwood staircase with a broken bannister and a rift in the middle led to the upper level on the left, just inside the entrance. Old paisley paper curled and lifted from the walls, revealing cracked plaster and the stain of paste long since eaten by American cockroaches. A smell kicked up from the decomposing carpet, like that of mould mixed with stale vodka and industrial cleaning products. Room 6 was the third on the right, at the back of the house, on the ground floor. Yes, there was a fibre mat, and under it, a key. She tried the key in the lock and pushed on the door, which creaked loudly on its rusty hinges as it swung open.

In spite of the tremor, Jade found an old brown Bakelite switch just inside the right hand door frame. It was gratifying that the light came on, although it was a bare bulb, hanging on a cloth-covered cord coming directly out of a discoloured plaster ceiling rose. There was a queen-sized bed in a wooden frame. A window, dressed with lace curtains, was set behind it, just above the bed-head. The light from the Laundromat shone through, projecting a silhouette of the old garden shed that stood just inside the fence. The bed was made up with plain sheets, pillows and a red doona with orange sunbursts. On the left of the bed was a tall open cupboard with hanging space. The locked door beside it led to stairs down into the garden, visible through the window. On the other side of the bed, there was a small low table with a toaster, an electric jug, two coffee cups, and a small gas burner attached to a cylinder underneath. Through the wall to the right, an open door led to an en suite bathroom with a toilet, a shower enclosure, and a basin with a dripping tap.

Jade stepped across the threshold, closed the door behind her and placed her bag inside the cupboard. She took off her shoes and lay down on the bed to wait for Nick as instructed. From where she lay, facing the door, she saw that a rack had been mounted on the wall to the right of the door. Hanging from it were various apparatus: handcuffs, a riding crop, a leather hood, a rope, and a short-handled cat-o'nine-tails.

*

Ned turned sharply into Harcourt Street and pulled the XR6 up abruptly beside where the garden shed stood, just through the fence, towards the back of the house. Nick jumped out of the passenger seat, vaulted the fence and went up the stairs to unlock the back door into room 6, causing Jade to jump right out of her festinating skin. 'Come downstairs and say hello to Uncle Ned!' Nick pushed her out in front of him. 'Stand there on this side of the fence.' Nick climbed back over.

Ned got out of the ute, walked around to the tail, dropped the gate and, with Nick's assistance, hauled out what seemed to be a long roll of old carpet, secured with straps at both ends, with a substantial bulge in the middle.

The redhead on the corner pretended not to notice.

The two men lifted the carpet onto their shoulders and walked to the fence. Nick ordered Jade to take one end as they pushed it halfway across the fence. Then he vaulted the fence again and asked Ned to push as he took the middle. Nick motioned to Jade to step back slowly as Ned eased the mass along, feeding more to Nick as he went.

Then Ned jumped over and took the rear.

Nick replaced Jade at the front and ordered her to take the middle. Nick led them around the back of the house to the other side of the plastic temporary fence to the construction site on the other side, where they stopped by the dark green industrial bin. Nick told Jade to leave the weight to him and Ned, to go round and lift the lid of the bin. Nick and Ned pushed the carpet into the almost empty bin. It fell with a thud.

Jade dropped the lid.

The construction zone at the back of the house was otherwise quiet. There was no light, and no sign of anything stirring in the yard.

Nick told Jade to get back inside and wait. 'We'll bring you something soon.' He returned with a long black wig, a little tartan miniskirt, a white spandex crop top, and a pair of high black boots. He tossed them at her. 'Here, strip and get this gear on! You're working for me now, bitch! And if you want a fix, you can give Uncle Ned here his reward, while I mix up!'

*

Late Friday afternoon, just as he was preparing to drive out of the hospital's basement car park, Garrick's phone rang. He picked up and answered, 'Garrick Willis?'

'Dr Willis, Sergeant Tammy Moroney here, from New Farm CIB.'

'Yes, Sergeant?' Garrick was already apprehensive.

'I'm afraid we may have some bad news for you. Are you on your way home at the moment?'

'I was just about to leave the hospital to head out to meet a friend.'

'I suggest you call your friend to say you've been delayed. Drive home, and perhaps call up a support person to be with you. We will drop around in about half an hour to talk. It's not something I'm prepared to tell you on the phone.'

Now Garrick was really spooked. 'Yes, thank you, Sergeant. I'll do that, and I'll be expecting you at my place in about half an hour.'

'I'll be bringing my partner Senior Constable Graeme Dixon with me. You're at Highgate Hill?'

Garrick confirmed the address. He called up Rachel, who insisted she would come over and join him, rather than wait at the Chalk alone. He was about to suggest to her that she was not likely to be left alone for very long, but thought better of it and drove home to wait for the police. He parked the BMW, took off his tie and undid the top two buttons of his shirt, before taking the lift up to the unit.

Rachel was first to arrive. She hugged Garrick and kissed his cheek. 'Something's wrong?' she asked. 'The police?'

'Let me get you a drink. I've no idea, except they said they have bad news. They want to break it here at home. Hope it's not Jade.'

'Me too! You say things have soured between you two, since Saturday? And you've not heard anything since Sunday night?'

'No! And you?'

'Not a sound. It's not like her'

The doorbell rang. Sergeant Moroney, with her red hair and green eyes, reminded him immediately of someone. He couldn't quite place her. 'Senior Constable Dixon,' she said, introducing the tall man in uniform beside her.

Garrick shook hands and showed the police into the lounge. He introduced Rachel as, 'My work colleague.'

Tammy Moroney began by reassuring Garrick. 'Dr Willis, we're from CIB, but I want you to know that we are not interviewing you on the basis of suspicion that you might be involved in criminal activity. Rather, we are here to bring you news, rather unwelcome news, of the death of someone who may be of significance to you, and in the hope that you might be able to assist us with our investigation.'

Garrick looked at Rachel. She was agitated, biting her lip and clenching her fingers. 'Somebody I know has died?'

'Dr Willis, a woman's body was found in a dumpster on a New Farm construction site this afternoon. A woman with long black hair. We found a letter, with the body, stamped, sealed and addressed to you. Of course the letter is being held as evidence, but we have made a copy, and we thought it was best that we should deliver it to you personally.'

She handed him the note.

Dear Garrick

I want you to know that I often think of you and Sandy. Although I do not know you as well as I should, and I have not been there when you needed me, I am very proud of you, of both of you. I knew you had become a doctor, but it was not until I heard you speak at your Grandmother's funeral that I really was able to know just how smart you are, not just with a science, but with words and feelings. I hope that someday I may be able to show you who I really am, to speak to you about your brother, tell you why I left your father, why I cannot be any good as a wife, or as a mother. And I hope you will be able to show me the same kindness that you show to others, to be able to forgive me.

'Dr Willis, when did you last see your mother?'

Garrick had been bracing himself for the worst possible news, but somehow hadn't thought at all about Charmaine. And what was this about a brother? He glanced over at Rachel, seated in the recliner just to his right. She looked puzzled and perplexed, but also relieved. Tears were welling in the corners of her almond eyes. She seemed worried about him. Then he let the wave of horror rush over him like a grey tsunami.

'Well, I'm sure, but I thought I saw her at my grandmother's funeral in Lismore—let me see—eleven days ago, the Monday before last. She was standing near the doorway of the funeral home café. When I noticed her, she fled. I went after her, but she slipped away from me. Then I thought maybe I had seen a ghost. She was supposed to be in rehab with the Salvation Army down at Cobaki, the last I'd heard, but I don't hear from her that often. Mostly when she calls, she tries to hit me up for drug money.'

Dixon asked, 'What was your mother's name?'

'Charmaine, Charmaine Willis. At least that's what she used to be called. She was Charmaine Craig before she married Dad. She left us when I was four. Went off with some biker guy.'

'Is it possible that she may have had other children? asked Moroney.

'Well, there was my sister Sandy, two years younger than me, but she scarcely remembers Charmaine. She was too young. Others? I don't know about that.' For a moment an image of the photograph

131

he'd glimpsed in Myshkin's wallet flashed through his mind, but he dismissed the ridiculous notion well before it had a chance to form.

'Dr Willis,' said Dixon. 'Homocide have not yet been able to positively identify the woman whose body was found with this letter. If she was Ms Willis, then you would be the next of kin. Are you willing to come down to the morgue with us and take a look?'

Garrick's stomach tightened in a knot. His heart was lead. His limbs had swum a deep water race in a sea of molasses. 'How did she die?'

'Well, the coroner will decide that at the inquest,' said Moroney, 'but there were needle marks up and down both arms, and cigarette burns all over her thighs.'

'I suppose we better get this done,' said Garrick.

Rachel looked up as Garrick dragged himself to his feet. There was compassion in her gaze, and something that could even turn to love, given a nudge. 'Garrick, I'll wait here for you,' she said.

GROUNDS FOR SUSPICION

While the bad news was broken, a cold front blew through. The temperature outside dropped by several degrees, and the rain began to fall. Tammy Moroney drove the modified Toyota Aurion police vehicle over to the John Tonge Centre at Coopers Plains, Graeme Dixon seated beside her, Garrick Willis in the rear seat immediately behind her. The windscreen wipers worked efficiently, back and forth. Something sure and reliable in a cruel and arbitrary world.

The rain reminded Garrick of the weather leading up to the 1974 floods, when he was a boy, at which time most of Lismore and about a third of Brisbane had been underwater. He preferred to believe it was the weather that was making him feel uncomfortable, and not his destination, or what he was likely to find there.

The receptionist at the morgue unlocked the side door and showed them through. The technician moved operating theatre light to shine directly onto the covered face of the corpse.

'Are you ready for this?' asked Tammy Moroney.

Garrick nodded. There was a knot in his throat that he just couldn't swallow.

The technician lifted the face sheet. The face was grey, as corpses are, with long black hair. 'It's her,' said Garrick.

'Charmaine Willis? Your mother?' enquired Moroney.

'Yes,' said Garrick, gesturing to the technician to cover the face again. As Garrick signed the identification certificate, he asked, 'How long until the body can be released?'

'Well,' said the technician, 'Dr Gorman will perform the autopsy tomorrow. What happens after that will be up to the coroner, but due to the circumstances in which the body was found, it may not be for some time yet.'

'Will I be allowed to see the autopsy report?'

'Yes, the report can be released to family after it has been reviewed by the coroner, provided that there are no suspicious circumstances. In this case, as there may be, the coroner will review Dr Gorman's report and authorise him to discuss it with you, so long as that is not considered likely to compromise the investigation. We'll be able to let you know about that within a few days. Are there other family members to be notified?'

'Charmaine was an only child. Her parents have been dead for many years. So far as I know, there's only my sister Sandy in Dubai. I'll call her. Charmaine and my father were divorced more than thirty years ago. I'll tell him anyway.'

'I'll give you my card. If you or any other family member should need the service, we have counsellors available. Please contact me, and I'll arrange it.'

Garrick thanked the technician, who buzzed the receptionist to show them out. Dr Willis was not one for casting aspersions. Poor dress sense and limited interpersonal capacity may not have been key selection criteria for technical positions at this establishment, but it was clear that they were little hindrance to permanent employment. Taken in isolation, they were not sufficient grounds for suspicion that Charmaine's body might not be safe from unnecessary interference. When the receptionist arrived, Garrick turned to leave, flanked by Dixon and Moroney.

Garrick made his way up in the lift to the fifth floor and entered the unit. 'You're still here?' Garrick was surprised to find Rachel waiting for him.

'You were expecting otherwise? You're rather pessimistic for a man who keeps a stock of all the ingredients for Singapore noodles!'

'Thank you. Would you like a beer?'

'I wouldn't mind!'

He reached into the fridge and pulled out two stubbies.

'Do you have a cooler?'

Garrick glanced up at his lone Sir Leslie Patterson insulation sleeve and decided that while Les might have his place in this kitchen, this was not his time. 'No, sorry, I don't.'

'I'll have a glass then.'

Garrick reached up into the cabinet and pulled down a crystal tumbler, part of his small share of the wedding spoils. Penny had kept all the furniture. He poured for Rachel, and drank straight from the stubby. 'Well, we get to share a drink after all!' He clinked his bottle against her glass.

Rachel brought the wok over and set it down on a bamboo chopping board, protecting the surface of the table. 'And you get to taste my noodles!' She paused, and looked him in the eye, rather coyly. 'Did you know that the stubby holder was invented in Canada?'

'Bullshit!'

'No, really. But the Americans call them *koozies* and imagine they came about due to their own genius sometime in the 1980s.'

'My Dad and his mates wouldn't touch a beer without one in the seventies. They were made out of styrofoam then. It's a bit like Grandpa used to say about the Melanesian boys diving from the peer at Port Morseby during the Second World War ...'

'Yeah? How so?' Rachel was intrigued.

'Well, a Yank would throw a penny in the water, and the boys would dive for it. Never mind the sharks. The Yank would say to Grandpa, "Gawd! It's a miracle the sharks don't eat them boys." Grandpa would come back and say, "All the boys have 'America won the war!' tattooed on their butts. Even the sharks won't swallow that!"'

Rachel giggled.

Garrick smiled for the first time in days.

Rachel served the steaming noodles into pasta bowls.

Garrick took another sip of his beer, picked up his chopsticks and twirled them to pick up a load before transferring them into his mouth. It did not surprise him that Rachel managed this more neatly than he could, but he was surprised to find himself the object of her affection. They continued to devour the noodles, each pausing occasionally for another swig of Cooper's.

Garrick finished his stubby. He noticed that Rachel's glass was still half full. He took another beer from the fridge and sat down beside her again. He felt the pressure on his calf again.

Rachel reached over and took hold of his left hand. She looked into his pale blue eyes and asked, 'How was it?'

Garrick began to shake, and then to cry.

*

Jade woke to the sound of rain pounding on the iron roof of her grandmother's cottage in Princess Street. After the dream, with its wild carnival of railway station buskers, walk-in roadside stalls for psychoanalysis, burlesque police inspectors, and rock-tart amateur porn stars intent on disembowelling her with shivs fashioned out of fractured plastic ice cream containers, it was a relief to be able to make out something familiar in the room. The high window above the French doors that led out on to the side verandah allowed just enough moonlight to enter.

That was as good as it would get. Jade was naked, cold and painfully stiff. Her teeth were chattering. It was difficult to tell where the shivering stopped and the involuntary twitching started. Someone had rubbed her eyeballs with sandpaper until their skin was so thin that they were about to explode. Her throat was stinging and dry as a hyena's laugh. Her shoulders had been torn halfway out of their sockets. They were behind her head, her arms tied together, stretched out straight-elbowed and secured to the pole that held up the mosquito net tester. Her legs were splayed open, tied at each ankle to the ornamental posts at the foot of the bed. Her skin crawled. Her nose was bleeding, and her pubic hair was clotted and matted.

The relief at familiarity receded quickly. Jade plunged into a state of conviction that her father had risen from the grave and was walking down the hallway to revisit his childhood room, where he would be so affronted at the state in which he, the undead, would find his daughter, that he would flee from the house, run back and forth across the road all the way down Main Street, heedless of the traffic, until he reached the Story Bridge. He would stop, just a little past half way over, just on the Fortitude Valley side. There he would mount the rail, raise his hands to the sky, roar fiercely, as the undead do, and launch himself once again to be broken on impact with the brown river so far below.

Footsteps came down the hallway. The handle turned and the door creaked open. Jade screamed.

'Quiet, little lady! I've brought you something to eat.' Nick threw the plastic carry bag with a KFC Dinner Box on to the bed.

'Untie me!' she pleaded, straining on the pantyhose, tears streaming down her face.

'Well, I'll do that if you'll hurry up and shower, eat some chicken, put on your little tartan skirt and your black wig again. Daddy'll fix you up then, cos he needs to get his girl back out to flog her arse on Main Street.

A NEW BEGINNING

When Garrick woke, Rachel had gone. His gaze drifted to the space beside him, to the indentation she left in the pillow. He found himself wishing that she was still there and that he could reach out to hold her. They hadn't made love, just lay in the bed together and held each other. The shock of his mother's death so fresh. Garrick was hoping Rachel was all right, that she had not left early in a panic, waking so close to a man after the horror of her recent rape.

Was it like this for Leonard Cohen, the day he composed his *Hallelujah*? Garrick was a poet, but no musician. Someone else must sing for him, so let it be Leonard.

And what of Jade? Jade, whom he and Rachel had so easily forgotten? Where was Jade now? Was she alone? Was she safe? Would she return? And who would she be, and what would they be, when she did?

Garrick knew he didn't care as much as he should. He forced himself to cut off these ruminations that could destroy the lightness and hope that came when he thought of Rachel and her kindness last night. With Jade, it had been a wild ride. Sometimes it had been a joyride, and at other times, it had been incredibly painful. Being with Jade was like riding the rollercoaster at Dreamworld. He sat next to her in the carriage, strapped and bolted in tight, their knees touching, his right hand high on the inside of her bare thigh, his left hand clutching tight on the safety bar as they peaked at the top of the ride, screaming together as they plummeted into the drop. At the end, it was a relief just to be able to get off.

In the shower, Garrick thought of those he must telephone with the news about his mother. It was not a long list: Dad, Sandy in Dubai— who else was there? Charmaine's parents had been killed in a car accident just a few weeks before she and Don had married. There was no one else that he could think would be interested. No, that wasn't true. He'd better call the Salvos who ran the rehab at Cobaki. They had been kind to her. They had given her the best chance she'd had. And they might know who else should know. They might have numbers. But it was always him they called when she was breaking out, about to be thrown out, or overdosing and being sent to hospital. As though he was her dad, and not that she was his mum. Well, she always put him down as next of kin. There probably wasn't anyone else who had cared. Maybe a dealer somewhere would weep at the loss of a regular customer. Strange, to think that she was really gone, and there'd be no more desperate late night calls. On the slab there, at the John Tonge Centre, she had seemed so small, so grey, so old. Fifty-seven, but somehow, like a dead child. Like his dead child.

Then Garrick thought of Tom, something he didn't do often enough. He paid his child support regularly, and once a fortnight he took the little fellow overnight, but he wasn't much of a father. He wished he could feel a stronger bond with his son, but somehow it just wasn't there. Could parental capacity be made or built, or was it just something that you have, or you don't have? *I'd better try harder, make a better effort. Like that little train engine in the book, the one that could.*

Garrick shaved and rinsed under the shower. He towelled himself dry, brushed his teeth, put on his bathrobe. He wouldn't be able to face those calls without coffee, although the longer he put them off the worse it would be.

Then he noticed the letter, on the kitchen table, weighed down by a chocolate heart, wrapped in red foil:

Dear Garrick

Sorry to leave early this morning. Must get home to change for work. It's very sudden, and a difficult time for you, but I was really glad to be with you last night. Could this be a new beginning?

Rachel xxx

*

Nick took the call lying down. *Who the fuck'd be calling me this time on a Saturday morning?* The digital display on his iPhone read 10.00. There was plenty of light streaming in from the little window high up on Jade's bedroom wall. So maybe it wasn't such a bad call after all. 'Nick here!'

'Dave here, Nick! Listen, I'm duty manager today, but something's come up. I need to get away at lunch time, do an insurance job for Wah-wah Bui. Can I ask a favour? Get in here and take over on the door until 11.00 tonight? Gina's on from then.'

'Yeah, okay Dave! I can manage that.'

'Another thing … I sent Tanya home. Seems she'd spent the night in the watch house. She's covered in bruises and still throwing up. Not a pretty sight when she's swinging out on a pole. So we're short on talent today. You know any girl that'd like to pick up a casual shift? Doesn't need to get up on stage, just to lap dance.'

'Dave, I think I have the girl for you! I'll bring her down.'

'Good on ya, Nick! We'll give her a go, and if she's any good with the customers, we'll keep her on. I'll let you train her.'

'See you at twelve then!'

Nick hung up and tossed the phone onto Jade's side of the bed, then shook her awake. . 'Wake up! Daddy's got work for you. Go and have a shower and get yourself cleaned up. We're spending Saturday at the Blue Velvet.'

*

'Dad, it's Garrick. Are you okay to talk?'

'What is it?'

'You got somewhere you can sit down?'

'That bad?'

'Bad as it gets. It's Charmaine ...'

Don had been anticipating such a call for many years now. At times Charmaine had turned up at the house at Goonellabah, raving and off her face. Don had to call the police, and eventually he established a permanent restraining order. Just the same, that didn't stop the occasional call in the early hours, when she would plead with him to come down and bail her out of the Lismore watch house. He'd been glad when, eventually, her attachment to him faded, and the emergency calls passed on to Garrick. Just the same, he was sorry for his son. 'Yes, go on.'

'She's dead, Dad. I went down to the morgue to identify her body last night. Some workmen found her rolled up in a carpet in a waste bin out the back of a construction site in New Farm. She'd been shooting up. They don't know whether someone had been hurting her, or if she'd started to mutilate herself again, but she had cigarette burns all over. I don't know. Maybe she overdosed and her dealer or whoever she was with panicked and decided to dump her.'

'That's terrible. It was bound to happen someday. Just a matter of time. It's a wonder she lasted this long. I'm sorry, though, for you. Does Sandy know?'

'I didn't feel up to calling anyone last night, after the time at the morgue. And she's six hours behind us. So I'll call her when we're through. It'll be early morning over there.'

'Well, I hope you can catch her. It's my guess it'll be all over the front page of the *Sunday Mail* tomorrow. It's a wonder the police have managed to keep the press off it so far. I'd hate to think of her finding it on the internet. Do you have any idea when they'll release the body?'

'No, Dad. That'll be up to the coroner. They'll notify me, when they have the autopsy report. I don't really feel like putting on much of a funeral. And she's got no other family. I wonder if you might come with me when they release the body, and we'll have her cremated. If Sandy can't get out for it then, we could keep the ashes, and we could scatter them together sometime later.'

'Charmaine lived a hard life. Can't say I've got much feeling for her now, except maybe relief that she won't be troubling us again. But I'm very sorry, son, and I'll be there for you if you need me to do that.'

'Thanks, Dad! I'll need to take you up on that, when the time comes.' Garrick ended the call, then tried to get through to Sandy.

After the usual sequence of pips for international calls, Garrick listened to the dial tone ring three times at the other end. 'Alo!' A male voice answered.

'Who's that? It's Garrick Willis here, in Brisbane, in Australia. Is Sandy there, my sister? May I speak to her, please?'

'She is sleeping. Please call back later.'

'I need to speak to her. It's about her mother.'

'It is very early and she is sleeping.'

Garrick heard the click at the other end as whoever it was put an end to the conversation.

*

Jade remembered when she was a nursing student, going to the late nineteenth-century building that now housed Blue Velvet, to see Michelle Shocked, when the club was Van Gogh's Earlobe. Michelle had grown her hair long, and appeared on stage in a dress. She sang *Cotton Eyed Joe, Come a Long Way* and *Anchored Down in Anchorage*. She delivered some great acoustic sets, but it seemed as though motherhood had just about knocked the skateboard punk rocker out of her.

Soon after that concert, the live music venue closed, and a franchised branch of a Fortitude Valley strip club called Bad Girls replaced it, taking the building back closer to its original function as the site of brothels serving the wharfies and sailors of the old South Brisbane docklands, and the resident doctors at the Mater Misericordiae Hospital. Subsequently the club had changed hands several times and was now trading under a new name, although the name on the licensee's plate had only recently changed after Henri de Brioche's involvement in a hydroponic enterprise in the Numinbah Valley was splashed across page three of the *Courier Mail*.

These fragments raced through Jade's mind as the methamphetamine accelerated on the bends of her veins, skidding across the feeling that she would otherwise have had as she gyrated, for the first time, around a silver pole on stage—that of being somewhat overexposed.

*

Garrick located Rachel in his contact list and pushed the call icon. The ringtone sounded seven times before going through to message bank.

'Thank you for calling Rachel Flanaghan ...'

Garrick waited for the end of the message, then hung up.

A few moments later, the phone rang back. 'Hi honey, sorry I missed your call. I was in the shower, just freshening up after work.'

'I'm calling to say thanks for your note. It was very moving. And to thank you too, for being there for me. I've been glad to have the opportunity to begin to know you. I'd love to see you again, too.'

'Well how about a movie this evening then?'

'I've got Tom, so not unless it's G rated, over here, and available on DVD.'

'Well, if you think it's okay, I'd love to meet him.'

'I'll cook for you this time!'

'Great! I'll look forward to that. But I won't sleep over this time. Maybe another time soon?'

'Well, let's see how we go? I'm on my way over to Penny's to pick him up Tommy now. We'll grab a movie at Civic Video. So how about you come over around 5.30? Do you like dry red peanut curry of chicken?' It was something he knew he could cook quickly.

'I'll try anything once!'

Tom loved the smell of the seats in his father's car. Usually he felt safe with the black leather around him, but today Daddy was strange. Maybe something was wrong. As he sat strapped into his plastic booster seat just behind Garrick, Tom stared out the window at the pylons of the Grey Street Bridge flashing by and said, 'Daddy, what's a Char-Main?' He had heard Garrick and Penny whispering.

'Charmaine was a lady Grandpa used to know, a lady who has died.'

'What's died, Daddy?'

'It means she's gone, and she won't be coming back.'

'So Char-Main won't be coming back?

'Tom, Daddy's going to cook Thai curry for dinner. Would you like that?'

'No, Daddy! Pineapple pizza!'

'Okay, Tom, we'll order one at Dominos, and get a movie while the pizza's being made.'

'Why not eat pizza?'

'Not tonight, Tom. Tonight we have a guest, and Daddy is cooking for her.'

'Will Aunty Jade be coming?'

'No, Tom. Aunty Jade won't be coming.'

'No Aunty Jade? Aunty Jade's nice. Why won't Aunty Jade be coming?'

Garrick said, 'Aunty Jade has gone away, and she won't be coming tonight.'

'Aunty Jade gone away? Not coming back? Has Aunty Jade died? Like Grandpa's friend Char-Main?' Tom burst into tears.

Garrick pulled up outside Dominos in Boundary Street, opened the back door, unclipped Tom's belt and lifted him from the booster seat, up across his shoulder. Tom thumped his father's back and screamed. 'Bad Daddy! Make Aunty Jade go away. Just like Char-Main! I want Aunty Jade!' The boy began to kick at Garrick's chest.

Garrick steadied himself, patted Tom gently on the back, and strode towards the doors of Dominos saying, 'Let's go and get that pizza, son.'

Once Tom was buckled back into the booster seat, behind his father, on the way down the road to the video store in Russell Street, he asked: 'If Aunty Jade's not coming, who is coming then?'

'Daddy's friend Rachel.'

'Who's Rachel? Why is she coming over?'

'Rachel is Aunty Jade's friend too.'

Garrick opened the car door, lifted the little boy out of his seat, put him down on his feet and took his hand. As they walked into Civic Video, Garrick asked, 'Should we get Bob the Builder again? Or Sponge Bob?'

'No Daddy, I want Wallace and Gromit!' Tom pointed to the case. 'That one, the one with Wallace and Gromit, and the Rachel monster!' Garrick picked up the case and walked to the counter to hire *Wallace & Gromit: The Curse of the Were-Rabbit.*'

Tom was quiet all the way back to the Dornoch Terrace unit. He insisted that he should carry the DVD, and that his father bring up his overnight bag, as well as the pizza. Once inside, he ran into his room and came out clutching the photo from Lone Pine. 'Will Rachel come with Daddy and me to see the koala?'

Garrick sighed and shrugged his shoulders. Suddenly he felt old, and not very wise. 'I don't know, Tom. Sometimes Daddy just doesn't know. Would you like some lemonade?' He poured the Sprite into a lime green Tommee Tippee sippy cup, sat Tom on the couch in front of the television, slipped the DVD into the machine and pushed play, before retreating to the kitchen.

Garrick lit the wok burner on the gas range. He took two chicken breasts from the fridge, drew his kitchen knife from its scabbard and cut them into two centimetre cubes. The flesh was pale and bloodless. A flash of the old imagery came momentarily, made him drop the knife. He countered it with a big red octagonal mental STOP sign, shook himself and pulled together. He picked up the knife and finished the job, poured a small volcano of cornflour onto a corner of the board, ground black pepper and sea salt into it, then rolled the chicken cubes in the mix one by one, plopping the first one into the cooking oil to check that it was warm enough to frizzle before going on. He continued until all the cubes were coated and beginning to crackle in the oil, as moisture evaporated. He dropped each one in by hand, copping an oil splash on the back of his left, just inside the thumb, below the index finger. He jumped back in pain, and was just about to run it under the cold tap at the sink when Tom toddled in, holding the cup with the dinosaur motif upside down, shaking it, proudly announcing: 'Sticky froth!'

'Shit!' yelped Garrick, as one of the chicken cubes deep-frying in the wok launched another pop of hot oil at almost the same spot on his hand.

Tom dropped the cup and fell on the floor wailing. 'I want sticky froth!'

Garrick jumped towards the sink, clutching the hand. He turned the tap on with his right and ran the left under it, his feet dancing like a man with prostatitis stuck too long in a queue for the urinal.

Tom flung the almost empty cup at his father, yelling 'Bad Dad!' from where he lay, kicking and flailing. Fortunately the wok of frying oil remained stably on the burner ring, crackling away as the doorbell rang. Garrick scooped up Tommy, still wailing, and went for the door, leaving the cold tap running.

Rachel was wearing a mandarin-collared emerald green silk dress. Garrick could smell *Opium*.

'Hello, gorgeous!' Rachel said to Tommy, who cautiously raised his head from where it was pressed against Garrick's chest and stared up into her face.

'I've got blue eyes. Aunty Jade had nice green eyes. You're eyes are like a cat! I don't like you!'

RENEWED FERVOUR

In the dream, Garrick was working undercover with the tall redhead. He wore a charcoal grey pin-striped suit with wide lapels, black pointy-toed patent leather shoes with white spats, a black shirt, wide suspenders, a white tie and a grey rabbit's fur Akubra fedora.

The redhead wore black leather hot pants and high stiletto lace-up boots. Her lashes were false black, with green eye shadow and a white zinc face. Her silk shirt was tied in a knot to reveal her slender waist, the sheen of fine velvet on her belly, her pierced navel roosting an articulated silver owl with yellow sapphire eyes. Her hair was aflame, and her lips were fire-engine red. She wore her police cap at a jaunty angle, and twirled a set of black steel handcuffs as a bracelet and chain on her right wrist.

She was a prostitute, and he was her pimp. And there were guns.

The redhead handed Garrick a stubby revolver, very much like an Arco No. 125 Sting toy hand gun, with *Made In Hong Kong* stamped into the metal over the trigger guard. He was a little boy playing gangsters with his wicked older sister.

She drew a standard police issue Glock Model 22 .40 calibre semi-automatic pistol, raised it to her rounded lips and blew across the tip of the barrel, turned to him and said, 'It's time for a reckoning, Dr Willis'. She gestured with the gun. He followed. They slowly raised their heads above the low sandstone wall, behind which they'd been crouching. They looked down into a street lit by pale gas lights.

On the corner, not ten metres from them, Myshkin was there, in profile, wearing his Commissioner's uniform, arresting a waif-like woman with long black hair hanging straight down her back. Her breasts were bare. She was naked apart from a red tartan micro-miniskirt, torn fishnets and black stilettos. When she turned her face to them, her blind green eyes stared at them like emeralds from the funeral mask of an ancient pharaoh. Her torso was mottled with black and yellow bruises. Blood poured from the wounds inside her left elbow where the fit had been dislodged, streaming down her forearm and dripping onto the pavement. Myshkin turned his back on them as he raised his baton to beat the junkie streetwalker all the way through the portal to the City of the Dead.

'You go first, Willis,' said the redhead.

Garrick cocked his gun, lifted himself up on to the wall and dropped down.

The sound of his landing brought Nick Myshkin face about.

Garrick raised the gun and pulled the trigger. A sputtering sound came from the barrel. A small lead pellet and something like the spring from a Parker pen dropped on to the pavement in front of him.

Myshkin's baton came down on Garrick's gun, scattering springs and ball bearings all over the street. Myshkin raised his baton to strike the girl again, as a bullet from the redhead's smoking Glock pierced his forehead and blew out the back of his skull, splattering his brains all over the streetwalker's long black hair.

Garrick woke with a jolt as a car exhaust on the street below his window backfired.

*

When the call came through, Tammy Moroney was in the driver's seat of a squad car up on the grass at Orleigh Park, next to the South Brisbane Sailing Club, parked under the branches of a gnarled old Moreton Bay fig. Sergeant Moroney's flame red hair hung down below her cap, and all the buttons of her uniform blouse were undone, exposing her silver chain with its crucifix and St Christopher medal that jangled as she tugged on the short lead attached to the dog collar around Senior Constable Dixon's neck, dragging his mouth down towards her left breast.

What were the New Farm CIB doing at 7.30 p.m. on a Saturday evening around the bend on the wrong side of the river, far away from the fleshpots of Brunswick Street and the dogging beats that they could otherwise be patrolling in New Farm Park? At this time, when off duty, Moroney would normally be found among the congregation emerging from early evening mass at Holy Spirit church, thanking Father O'Flaherty for the sermon, then home to her Merthyr Road unit to change and head out clubbing.

Just above the patrol car, a flying fox launched itself from the upper branches of the fig and took flight towards Toowong, startling Dixon

His teeth clenched involuntarily, earning a harsh jerk on the lead and a slap on the right cheek.

'Bad dog!' exclaimed Moroney, pulling herself away from him as the radio chirped and crackled.

*

Calliope was working late that Saturday. Dave was the last customer to leave the salon at around 6.45 p.m., losing his beard and shedding all his hair except the rat's tail. Cally sent Spiro off to meet his mates at the Wickham, called up Thanh Le's to order herself spring rolls with rice vermicelli salad, swept the floor of the salon, tidied up the magazines, and slipped next door to collect her take away.

Dave was still out the front, rummaging about in the back tray of a Ford XR6 utility truck parked three doors down from the restaurant. He hefted a can of mower fuel out onto the pavement, as Cally walked by with her bowl in a white plastic bag. Dave watched her for a moment from behind as she turned towards the salon.

Once inside, Cally locked the front door, slipped into the office down the back, pulled a bottle of ouzo out of the fridge and settled down to a date with her small business accounting package.

*

Jade was dancing in pink lingerie, on the lap of a stocky Vietnamese man in his late twenties, in a room out the back of the Blue Velvet. He smiled at her placidly as she leant down to whisper in his ear and rattle out the no touching rule. For a moment, she wondered if she had seen him at the Princess, but she rapidly dismissed the thought and carried on encouraging him. *He's just like the little fat man with the laughing mask, the one who runs out in front of the lion dancers at Chinese New Year, the one who shakes the coin collection box.* Her mind raced on, leaping from one association to another, exploding like a string of poha firecrackers. He clamped his hands onto her breasts, pulling her down hard, thumbs and forefingers twisting her nipples.

Jade screamed, and Nick burst in through the curtains, brandishing a pair of sticks joined by a short chain. Hoa Bui lifted his left hand from

153

Jade's breast and held her to him tightly round the waist as he reached down with his right and pulled a Smith & Wesson double-action .45 ACP semi-automatic from his ankle holster, flicked off the safety catch and pointed it at Nick's head.

Jade was momentarily silent. 'Don't stop talking dirty, baby,' said Hoa. 'It soothes me. Calms me when I'm trigger happy.'

'Wah-wah Bui! You fucking little prick! You're gonna get yours for that stunt you pulled on me in the Neuro lab!' yelled Nick, raising the weapon behind his head.

'Yeah, you pissed and shat yourself when you fitted! What else can you do for tricks? Drop the nunchaku before I blow your fucking brains out.'

Nick obliged, mindful of the Smith & Wesson.

Hoa shoved Jade over towards Nick. He pointed the gun in her direction. 'Bruce Lee's gonna give me a head job.' He beckoned to Nick with his left hand.

Jade watched as Nick kneeled, unzipped Hoa's jeans and went down. 'Do it good, and don't bite me, bitch, or you'll never deal in my Dad's clubs again.' He gestured to Jade, 'You can go now, girlie!' and put the barrel of the gun against Nick's temple, caressing him with the metal as he bobbed up and down.

With Bui's gun in that position, Nick turned to his task with renewed fervor.

Jade bowed slightly, turned and slipped out through the curtain to the bar.

*

Dave had the pantyhose pulled over his face, with the nylon legs hanging down his back. He laid his gun down on the doorstep, splashed most of the petrol over the wall behind Than Le's kitchen, then tilted the can upside down to use the last of it to dowse a pile of cartons leaning against the gas cylinders by the mini-skip. He pulled a zippo and a cigarette from his pocket, struck a light, took a drag and threw the smouldering durry into the mix, dodging the whoosh as he grabbed the gun and bolted through the door into the crowded restaurant.

There were screams and a few gunshots, then it all went up, with a bang.

*

Under the Moreton Bay fig, the radio crackled inside the squad car. Another bat dropped guano on the windshield, as Sergeant Moroney answered the call and quickly buttoned her blouse. 'There's a shooter at a restaurant fire!' she told Dixon. 'Kitchen's exploded.' She turned the key in the ignition of the supercharged Toyota, then hurtled along the back streets, coming to a screeching stop outside Thanh Le's just as Dave burst out the front door, brandishing a sawn-off Mossberg pump action shotgun. Moroney sprung out the driver's door and lunged for him.

Dave blew her away before she could draw.

Then Dixon hit Dave's right shoulder with a burst from his Glock.

Dave was standing over the fallen officer, grinning stupidly, as bright red blood pumped liked a fountain out of the sizeable hole in Moroney's chest. Dave fell as Dixon's gun spat, blowing holes in his head.

Somewhere, in a place far away, Constable Dixon was imagining what he would say to the coroner when his dental records revealed a perfect match with the bite marks on what was left of Moroney's breast. Dixon reached up with his free hand to remove the dog collar that was still fastened around his neck.

The refrigerators in the kitchen exploded, sending a fireball through to the front of the restaurant, showering Dixon, Dave and Moroney's corpse in a million fragments of glass.

Dave was still twitching.

Dixon squeezed the trigger on the Glock. As the first fire engine and the paramedics screamed down the street, Dixon pulled the trigger again.

*

On Monday, back at the Queensland Brain Institute, Garrick found he was able to throw himself into the laboratory work with new energy and zest. He opened his email to find news of ethics committee approval for a modification of his clinical research trial protocol. After a sad run of recidivism in the shoplifters, culminating in the loss of his favourite Parker pen, his iPhone and the screws that held his computer workstation together, he had been dying to replace Kubrick's *A Clockwork Orange* with a new weapon, hitting the bastards with a full three hours of deterrent dysphoria.

Hoa Bui seated the three subjects in their chairs, capped and wired-up them up, and strapped them in securely as Garrick watched from behind the observation screen. Garrick waited for Hoa to give the all clear signal, then pushed the button on the console to project

David Lynch's *Inland Empire* on to the theatre screen. If three hours of Hollywood starlets falling out of haunted screen sets down rabbit holes, accompanied by ninety decibels of dystonic roaring wasn't enough to set the shoplifters' guts churning, then having the actors stalk each other through shanty towns until one is disembowelled with a Phillips screwdriver would have to turn the trick. Not to mention the finale, back in the mansion, where all join hands like sisters with the rabbits and break out into Bollywood dance.

Garrick watched the multiple EEGs on the electronic monitors for a while, then reached for the *Courier Mail* that Hoa had left lying on the bench. He'd spent the afternoon cleaning up at home yesterday after dropping Tom off at Ascot, so he hadn't caught up with the news. The front page headline read: 'THIRTY DIE IN WEST END RESTAURANT BLAZE: Police Say Worst Since Whiskey Au Go Go'. Garrick turned to Hoa and asked, 'This wasn't your Dad's place was it?'

'No,' said Hoa, 'they were friends of the family.'

'That's terrible. I'm sorry that all this has happened.'

'Well, maybe not good friends!' Hoa was grinning.

Why's he so happy about it? I wonder what he's up to ... he's a hard one to make out, thought Garrick, turning back to his paper to read on a little further, alarmed to discover that a policewoman had died at the scene, a shotgun blast through the heart, point blank. She and the man who'd shot her down were now lying side by side on trays in the morgue with Charmaine.

The policeman who'd taken out the gunman had been transferred to the Toowong Private Hospital for psychiatric treatment after minor burns, cuts and abrasions were attended to at the Princess Alexandra

Hospital emergency department.

The fire had spread to the hairdressing salon next door, where a valiant fireman had carried out the proprietor from the back office, recently asphyxiated, overwhelmed by smoke inhalation. Paramedics had attempted to resuscitate her. She'd had a pulse when the ambulance left to take her to hospital, but she succumbed on the short journey, and was dead on arrival.

Poor Cally! Garrick could not bear to take in any more of the story. He didn't flip towards the end of the paper where, on the obituaries page, he might have read the official version of the life of the soon-to-be posthumously decorated Sergeant Tammy Maroney.

Garrick was emotionally numb. He mooned his way through clinic and ward rounds, dodging the horror by worrying instead about whether things were going too fast with Rachel, who'd called when he was on the way to work, inviting him over her place for a run and a swim before dinner. She'd suggested he might also bring a change of work clothes, in case he decided to take up her offer to spend the night.

SHADOW

Garrick rang the buzzer at the entrance to Rachel's tower in the Story Apartments. He was carrying a change of work clothes, his swim goggles and speedos, his bathrobe, his toiletries bag, a bottle of wine and his running gear, all in a black Adidas sports bag. In his other hand he held a bunch of red roses, purchased hurriedly at Coles. He nervously moved from one foot to the other. This was the first time he had been to Rachel's for a sleep-over.

'Who's there?'

Garrick jumped when Rachel's voice came from the intercom.

'It's me, Garrick!'

'You were really weird in the ward round today. You'd better tell me what's up. It's unit 7, on the second floor.'

Garrick shared the lift with a blonde woman whom he judged to be in her early forties, coming up from the car park below, dressed in lycra three-quarter pants, a red sports bra, and brand new runners. She glowed a healthy orange without runnels, direct from the tanning studio. Garrick could detect no sign that she had shed a drop of sweat.

She smiled at him and commented on the scent of the flowers. 'You can bring those to me on the fourth floor anytime you like, darling!' she told him, as he alighted at the second floor.

Garrick blushed and stuttered as the lift doors closed.

Rachel met him at the door. She was already dressed to run, in an outfit almost identical to that worn by the blonde woman in the lift, right down to the Mizunos. Fluorescent pink socks and little shorts with a red tie at the front were the only differences. Rachel had a frown on her face, but lit up with delight at the sight of the roses. She burst out laughing. 'You really are an idiot, aren't you? Are those for me? They're lovely!'

Garrick was perplexed. He often felt like one, but he wasn't quite sure why she should be calling him an idiot just now, or how it was that bringing roses qualified him.

She reached out to take the flowers, embraced him warmly and kissed him on the lips.

'I hope you've brought your running gear,' she said, ushering him into the bedroom. 'Hurry up and get changed!'

Garrick put down the Adidas bag, unzipped it, pulled out a bottle of Kabiminye Kerner, 2010 vintage and passed it to her. 'My favourite vineyard,' he said, 'in the Barossa Valley. You'd better chill it.'

'Really? Lighten up! I thought I'd put it in the microwave instead, and see how long it takes to explode.'

'That's a bit difficult after what I saw in the paper today. I had to write a poem about it. I want to show you …'

'We can talk about it while we run. And then I want to get you in the pool. You can show me the poem later.'

Garrick pulled on his black shorts, a bright orange shirt, white socks, a yellow cap, prescription sunglasses and blue runners. He wasn't really one for colour co-ordination. Leave that for the girls. Real runners dressed for comfort.

Soon Garrick was panting, as Rachel glided down the O'Connell Street hill, shuffling and clumping along as fast as he could behind her, regretting that 10 kilogram tyre he'd put on around his waist since the last time he'd run the Gold Coast half marathon. They crossed over the foot bridge at Dockside, took a right turn to run past the marina, a left at the ferry terminal and on along the boardwalk by the river, past the spot where the catamaran had breached the boardwalk wall and grounded during the floods. Many of the boards were still loose, and some of the paving bricks stood up a fraction on the walkway further on. Otherwise, no signs remained of the inundation.

'So what is it?' she said, as he managed to come up beside her, just before they ran into Captain Burke Park and up to the drinking fountain under the Story Bridge.

'Did you see in the *Courier Mail*, about the fire at Thanh Le's? That was my hairdresser who died in the salon next door.'

'And did you see, in the obituaries, that Sergeant Moroney, who took you to see Charmaine on Friday night, was the one gunned down on Hardgrave Road?'

'Shit, no! I didn't get that far into it. I was knocked about thinking of Calliope, the hairdresser. She seemed to have a bit of a thing for me. Poor woman. I couldn't get it out of my head, her amazing blue-green eyes. In the poem ...'

'Shut up and run. You can show it to me when we get home.' They ran up to the ferry terminal next to the Jazz Club, then turned and ran all the way back again. 'Let's cool off with a swim,' said Rachel.

'Can I show you the poem first?'

'All right, so long as you get changed straight away. I've bought a new brazilian bikini and I want you to tell me that it doesn't make my bum look big.'

'Okay,' said Garrick. They were already halfway up in the lift to the second floor. He walked into the bathroom and shed his running gear, pulled his black speedos out of the sports bag and grabbed his goggles.

He pulled out his hardcover bound account book, the one with a red cover, in which he drafted his poems during spare moments at work. This one hadn't even made it into a Word file yet.

Rachel emerged wearing the tiniest orange bikini Garrick had ever seen.

'Well?' she said.

'You look really nice in those togs. Just like Behati Prinsloo in the Seafolly posters. But I like your long black hair so much more.' Garrick hoped he had said something right. 'Now can I read you the poem?'

'All right, but be quick. I'm dying to get wet.'

Garrick opened the notebook and read aloud:

Shadow

My hairdresser's eyes
were delicate windows
with awnings shadowed
in fluorescent aqua
and fringed with lashes
of kohl black mascara.
I told her of fever
that burned in the seventies
for girls in the city
with blue eye shadow.
Their acrylic tipped fingers
wore an itch to scratch
less tender than hers
as she worked at the basin.

After the fire
that burned out the salon
my hairdresser's eyes
were blackened windows
to a shut down soul
still open for business
but closed to kindness.
I raked the embers
until I found words
to bring on grief's labour
in a basin of tears.
I have forgotten her name
but I won't forget the colour
of my hairdresser's eyes.

'Very nice,' said Rachel, with a sulky look. 'Maybe if she'd lived you would have read it to her, too. Maybe you'll write a poem for me some day.'

'I did, the day I first saw you. I fell in love with you across the room—with the tattoo on your shoulder.'

'And you delivered it to my table—to a total stranger!'

'I guess I can be a bit of an idiot.'

'Yes! And now that you know me, and I think I'm falling in love with you, I just keep hoping you'll do it again, and again—write me a poem, that is, not fall in love with a total stranger.'

'I'm working on it,' said Garrick, crestfallen.

'Now why don't you look into my eyes? Do they look like cat's eyes to you? Chinky?'

As the club was closing in the early hours of Sunday morning, Hoa gave Nick a gentle shove, with the barrel of his gun, out onto the sidewalk before pulling down the roller door and locking up. He turned to Jade, seated behind him on a bar stool, speeding away as she sipped on a cocktail of grenadier, blue curacao, and ice. She was wearing a short black satin bathrobe with a dragon embroidered on the back, and red stilettos. Her hands were jittering, shaking the glass and spilling the liquid as she turned around on the stool, swaying dangerously and threatening to tilt towards the floor.

'Would you like me to take you for a ride?'

'Whatever!' she said, intercepted by Hoa's arm around her waist as she attempted to rise from the stool and staggered to the right.

Hoa led her out the back of the club and half-carried, half-dragged her to the passenger side of the black Mercedes SLK convertible parked in the lane. He fastened her seat belt. By the time he'd made it to the driver's side, her head was lolling, and she'd fallen fast asleep. Noticing the goose flesh rising all over her body, and the bluing of its extremities, he reached behind the seat for a picnic blanket and threw that over her before driving the few blocks to his South Brisbane unit.

In the dream, Cally came to Garrick through a cloud of smoke, coughing and spluttering. She wore a transparent black negligee. Garrick found himself noticing things about her in a way that he had never imagined, in waking life, while she lived. Somewhere, a long way from Hendersonville, Johnny Cash was singing *Ring of Fire*.

'I wrote you a poem,' said Garrick-in-the-dream.

'But not until after I died,' reproached Cally. 'Heed me, Garrick Willis, for I have not long to tarry. The harbinger will follow me, bearing this message: Pay heed, lest you loiter, and vacillate, lest you invest too little, and love too late.'

Garrick-in-the-dream strained to reach out to her, but she faded and disappeared into the smoke, vanished leaving the scent of aniseed and an archaic rhyming couplet hanging in the air. He began to shiver. The heat that surrounded Cally's spectre was replaced by a moist, icy chill. What had seemed to be smoke now was fog, sticky and seeming to creep in tendrils up his trouser cuffs and down under his collar. When he reached to wipe his brow, he found it covered with droplets of condensation. Suddenly his eyes were blinded by a torch beam, seeming to originate from a spot somewhere beyond where Cally had appeared to fade, then disappear.

Garrick-in-the-dream blinked. As his pupils accommodated, he could make out a figure advancing towards him—that of a tall pale woman with flaming red hair hanging down in curls on either side of the peak of a police cap with a black-and-white chequered band. She was wearing high motorcycle boots with gaiters, and tight black leathers. She held the torch in her left hand, shining it insistently into his eyes. Her face was whited as though with the shit of a nightingale—a geisha effect in white zinc. Her lips were painted blood red, like those of the late Marcel Marceau. She held her right hand over her heart. When she raised it to command him to stop, a fountain rushed out from a gaping chest wound. Her black cycle gloves dripped fresh blood. The red stream bubbling from her thoracic lesion made the larger contribution to the gore, but it was joined by rivulets that ran from puncture wounds in the cubital veins inside the elbows of both arms.

'Turn, Garrick Willis,' she commanded in that same brown voice. 'You are too quick to forget. A friend in trouble is spurned too soon. You readily embrace the new, but with the gift, remember, something old with something new, and something tinged with a touch of blue. Death, too soon, will follow. Go now, or death will come, with you too late.' She picked up a long black wig and pulled it over her shock of red-as-Ronald-McDonald hair. As her left hand stretched towards him, placing a white rectangular wafer in his right, her face morphed into that of his mother on the mortuary slab. Then she was gone.

Garrick looked down into the palm of his hand with a sense of something vital coursing through his body, as though he had just received his first communion. On the middle of the rectangle, a blue plus sign was distinctly emerging.

Garrick woke with a jolt. Rachel turned restlessly in her sleep, pulled the sheets off and bumped him with her left elbow. The sweat was chill on his bare torso.

*

The spring sunshine streaming in across the balcony of the fifth-floor apartment at Riverview Gardens played on the sticky dust the Sandman sprinkled on Jade's eyes in the early hours of Sunday morning, when Hoa Bui carefully placed her in his bed, then lay down beside her to sleep.

It was the urge to pee that woke Jade, rather than the morning sun. She blinked as best she could, amidst the glue of mucus and mascara. She noticed Hoa lying prostrate on his back, snoring softly. She took in the burner, spoon and other apparatus on the bedside table and stumbled out to the en suite, where she found the seat up on the white ceramic pedestal. The smell of androstadienone is, for some, an aphrodisiac pheromone, but for Jade, this morning, it wrenched her guts. She retched, experiencing a desperate urge to flush. The water cascaded at the push of a button. She lowered the lid and sat down. Her swollen breasts hung down on her chest as she crouched. Unless it was yet another drug-related sensory distortion, she could swear that they were larger than they were a week ago, although she had eaten very little. They were sore and tender to touch.

Jade stepped into the shower, lathered herself and luxuriated in the soothing effect of warm water beating on her chest, running down across her navel. She emerged dripping wet, temporarily subject to the illusion of being clean again. She wrapped herself in Hoa's blue bath sheet, shook her hair like a wet dog, then picked up the bath mat from the floor and made it into a turban. She dried herself, wandered back into the bedroom and reached for dragon bathrobe draped over the end of the bed.

Hoa stirred, stretched, and opened his eyes. 'Hello, blondie!' he said.

'Would you please take me home?'

'Sure thing, pussycat. You'll need me to visit soon. I'll let you know when I have work for you.'

Rather than have Hoa drive her home to Toohey Street, where she hoped she might restore for herself a haven of separation between the worlds, she gave him the New Farm boarding house address. At Harcourt Lodge, he kissed her by the shed, and left her at the bottom of the short flight of back room stairs.

Later that morning she wandered down to the seven-day chemist at the Merthyr Road Shopping Village, where she bought a test kit. In the women's toilets under Vue restaurant, she passed a few drops of urine into the depression on the little white plastic rectangle, then watched the blue cross materialise distinctly out of the shadow cast by the rim, at the centre of the blot. She bought a cask of wine at Vintage cellars, trudged up Brunswick Street, and returned to her room. It was not until Tuesday that she could bring herself to charge her phone again and text Garrick for the first time since Father's Day.

Garrick tossed and turned, but couldn't get back to sleep. He had been in the midst of another dream, of which he could recall very little—something about a heart-shaped locket from which his mother's photograph had been removed. Nothing had replaced it, then an image of two little hearts, beating in synchrony, on an early foetal ultrasound. He blinked and looked around him in the street light that made its way through the window. He was a stranger to this apartment, and to everything in its space. Rachel's long black hair lay in a tangle on the pillow beside him. Even the down in the little curve that made up the small of her back was beautiful.

Garrick's iPhone rang, sounding the theme from The Twilight Zone. The screen showed 4.00 a.m., and Sandy's number.

'Sandy?'

'Garrick, why didn't you call me? I've just been talking to Dad.'

'I did call, on Saturday—early morning your time. The chap that answered wouldn't put you on—said you were sleeping. I told him it was urgent, and to tell you to call me.'

'Well, he didn't! I'm so sorry. I'll have to chew him out later.'

'What's his problem?'

'He's very jealous. Any time a man calls, he accuses me of sleeping around'.

'It's Charmaine. She's dead.'

'And you've had to go and identify the body, all on your own.'

'Well, not on my own, not strictly. A couple of police officers took me to the John Tonge Centre. But one of them has since been shot dead, and the other's been suspended, while they investigate him gunning down his partner's killer.'

'So how did Charmaine die?'

'Well, they haven't released the autopsy report yet. There will be a coronial inquest. She had track marks all over her. The police are treating the matter as homicide, but it was probably just a drug overdose. I'm guessing that her dealer fixed her up, then she arrested on him in his shooting gallery. He may have been off his face, and not tried to resuscitate her, or else he tried and failed. Either way, he had a corpse to deal with, and probably panicked.'

'She lived a wild life.'

'She never should've had kids. We're lucky we had Dad, and he was lucky Christine came along.'

'So what will we do?'

'Well, we have to wait for the coroner to say it's okay to release the body. That could be months away, given that the police will want to charge someone, at least with interfering with a corpse, if they can find the dealer.'

'Much chance of that?'

'Well, I think that Sergeant Moroney, the one that was shot, she must've been on to something. But now that she's gone, the investigation may be dropped—in which case, maybe a few weeks.' He paused, to clarify his thoughts. 'Moroney, the police sergeant who was killed, and Dixon, the constable—they're New Farm CIB. What were they doing, responding to a call at West End?'

'Does it matter?'

'Well if they'd been minding their own business, on their side of the river, she wouldn't have been killed.'

'She might just as well have been gunned down in any nightclub in the Valley.'

'Yeah, I suppose. But somehow, I think not. She seemed to me the kind of woman who knows how to keep everything under control.'

'I hope you're not looking for a dominatrix! You've got trouble enough on your hands with Jade.'

'We aren't together anymore. Things blew up on Father's Day, and I haven't heard from her since. She'd been more and more erratic over a few weeks, well before Grandma's funeral. And now I think she's been missing from work too. I've been worried about her, but she's texted forbidding me to check up on her, so I haven't gone round to her place. I hope she's all right. Anyway, I'm seeing someone else now ...'

'My poor brother! That's a quick move.'

'Well, maybe, but we've known each other for a while.' He looked around him, at the strange surrounds, and at the slender woman by his side, just beginning to stir from sleep.

'Well, I hope it turns out all right. I just don't like seeing you hurt. Let me know when they let us have the body, and I'll come out. Maybe we should have her cremated, and scatter the ashes somewhere?'

'Yes, it's hard to know what to do. No one knew her very well, not even Dad. He found out the hard way, just how little he really knew of her. I don't think she had any real friends, only dealers, and the men who used her. Maybe the Salvos—they were the ones who really cared about her. But she resented them and was always bucking the rules. Like she could never let the love get in.'

'Well, I'd better go now, brother. Ahmad's beginning to wonder why I'm taking so long.'

'Bye, sis! I'll call you as soon as I hear.' He hung up the phone just as Rachel turned to him with a puzzled look on her face.

'Who was that?

'Sandy, my sister, in Dubai.'

'Why's she calling at this horrible hour of the morning?'

'She's only just heard about what happened to Charmaine.'

'Didn't you tell her on Saturday?'

'I tried, but I couldn't get through.'

'Well, I could do with some more sleep. And I could use a cuddle. Are you coming back to bed?'

*

When Rachel was asleep again, Garrick gently dislodged himself from her arms and went and sat out at the dining room table. In the pale rose glow that was beginning to make its way in through the window from over the eastern reach of the Brisbane River, he took out his notebook and began to write:

> *locket*

> *entering the locket*
> *without a photograph*
> *father dreams*
> *the image*
> *of unborn children*

their hearts
pitter-patter
in and out
of synchrony

each swallow of the amnion
each kicking limb
alters the rhythm
of the little drums

they ride
the oscillation
of his thrusts
as mother shudders
drawing breath

*

On the long walk home from the Blue Velvet, Nick could still smell
gunmetal, and the taste of cum niggled at the back of his throat. He
looked up towards the statue on the roof of the Mormon Temple. He
could've sworn that the angel dipped his trumpet, wiggled its hips and
gave a little bow, in mock celebration of his oral defloration. He walked
up Main Street, past the Southern Cross Motel, and on to the Night
Owl where, on the corner opposite the Pineapple Hotel, there used to
be a woman in a tartan miniskirt, with long black hair streaming half
way down her back, restless and shivering, waiting for him to come

with his backpack, his rubber tubing and his kit, but there was no one, not even a wisp of mist. The breeze blew a grey plastic shopping bag across the street.

A bat took off towards New Farm from one of the ancient figs in the park. Tomorrow he would go to Bunnings to buy a brand new set of secateurs and a durable pair of oversized gardening gloves. The words of Neil Young's *Lost in Space* ran through his head. She was his, and he was nobody's bitch.

*

Garrick drove to his Dornoch Terrace unit after he finished his clinic, collected a fresh change of clothes and drove back to Rachel's. It was difficult to find a park on the streets among the unit towers at Kangaroo Point. He felt uneasy leaving his gleaming machine out in the open, so vulnerable to the hailstorm he expected might be brewing in those thunder clouds mounting, swelling up beyond the horizon somewhere out in Moreton Bay. It was blowing in, green and overbearing, an emerald menace in the sky, overshadowing the town.

Garrick lugged his Adidas bag up the ramp to the security door when the signal sounded on his iPhone. The text was from Jade: 'I'm sorry for what I said. I'm pregnant. Please help.'

The sky lit up with a flash. The thunderclap was almost simultaneous. The heavens opened and began to empty onto him as he collected his sensibilities to buzz for Rachel on the intercom. The father in the sky had spoken, with his hammer. That afternoon, in the gaps when patients failed to front, he had been reading Michael Ondaatje's *Divisidero*. He realised that Rachel might not be entirely pleased to hear this news of her old friend. He hoped that someone, somewhere, was watching over him, someone who would cradle him and know what to do. Just like the novelist, he was feeling the need for a father who would know what to do, the 'need for a lullaby, not a storm'.

*

All day Hoa Bui played with the key in his pocket. As he prepared the patients for their EEGs, as he wired them up, watched over their welfare, cleaned up after them, and printed the electronic traces of their brain waves, he smiled internally, smug with the knowledge that, once again tonight, he would be fucking the boss's girl and feeding her habit.

When the clock made half past four, Hoa took the lift to the ground floor, down past Pharmacy and Patient Enquiries, took a left turn at the florists, away from the main entrance. He walked past Starbucks, then on to the tunnel that led to the staff car park entrance. He pointed the remote at the Merc, enjoying the way the lights blinked at him. He was out the gate a minute later, drove home to collect the gear, then changed into a pair of baggy cargo pants and t-shirt. Back on the road again, he took a quick stop at McDonald's on Main Street to buy himself a burger and a Happy Meal for the girl before driving over the bridge and off towards New Farm.

*

The lift lurched to a stop halfway between the first and the second floors. Garrick's guts kept on rising, bashing rudely into his diaphragm before they thudded back down into their usual anatomical positions.

175

The light inside the lift flickered for a moment, went out, and then came back on again. A whirring noise entered from the lift shaft above, then there was a clunk, and the lift began to move once more. It came to rest with the doors open onto Rachel's corridor. Garrick was glad to get out.

Rachel greeted Garrick at the door, dressed in her running gear. Her stomach was taut, and perfectly flat. Her skin reminded him of the burnished rose gold found in engagement rings of the nineteen thirties, rings that could be scoured from antique stores and pawn shops. He remembered such a ring on the third finger of the left hand of a patient's corpse. He could not remember the wedding band.

In the moment before he embraced Rachel, Garrick thought of piercing her navel and setting an emerald jewel in it. The skin of her back, in the place between her shoulder blades, was silken as he held her tight, then ran his fingers up and down the mane of her long black hair, imbued with the scent of jasmine and lemongrass, as he returned her kiss.

'Why so grim in the face, Dr Willis?' she asked, releasing him. 'You look like you've just seen your poor mother's ghost!'

'It's Jade,' he said. 'I've just heard from her. She's in trouble.'

'Well, come in and tell me about it,' she said, walking over to sit on the couch and patting the cushion next to her.

Garrick sat down, took his phone out of his pocket and showed her the text.

'Is it yours?' asked Rachel.

'I don't know. She's made some strange friends lately, and she's had her secrets. I couldn't bear the outbursts anymore, and the taunts. I think she's been pumping it up her arm and I got to be pretty dull by comparison. Have you heard from her at all?'

'Well, she rang me at work on Thursday, asked me to tell administration that she was off sick and might not be back for weeks. I asked, 'Why don't you tell them yourself?' She called me a stuck-up bitch, screamed at me over the phone and then started crying. Mumbled something about a boarding house on the corner of Brunswick and Harcourt. Then the phone went dead.'

'Why didn't you say something before?'

'To tell you the truth, I've gotten sick of her antics myself, and I after all the drama with you and your mother and us getting together like this, so unexpectedly, it was driven out of my head. I guess I just didn't want to think about her.'

'I don't know what to do. We can't just leave her in this mess.'

'We?' She edged away from him a little, waving her hand in front of her delicate nose. 'By the way, you need to get out of that work shirt and take a shower.'

Garrick chose to ignore the latter comment, but took in the implication that, if Jade was pregnant to him, he had begun to stink for Rachel, maybe worse than Lazarus, rising after three days in the tomb. 'Well, I thought you were her friend. And it seems that now, more than ever, she needs friends.'

'Well, we're not going looking for her now!'

'I guess not,' said Garrick. 'I suppose I'd better get changed so we can go for a run, then get some dinner. Look! It's already bat o'clock.'

A squadron of leathery mammals crossed the patch of sky above the glimpse of the river that could be seen between the apartment towers, through the glass of Rachel's tall picture window.

A NIGHT IN THE TOOLROOM

It was just on five past ten when some gorilla of an ex-Valley Diehards front row forward gave Nick a shove out the side door of the public bar of the Empire Hotel, ripping the black Megadeath muscle shirt off Nick's back. He fell on the concrete drive and lay there swearing softly, clutching the neck of his brown paper bag into his belly and thanking God for saving the Stollie. His backpack followed him, hitting the pavement hard beside him, just missing his head.

Upstairs, Sydney DJs Sam Scratch and fRew were laying down the tracks, with the doof doof booming across the iron lace that bordered the verandah, spilling into the street. Nick held onto the Stollie with one hand, and onto his head with the other. He struggled up onto his wasted legs, discarded the remains of his shirt, picked up his backpack and staggered round the front to throw up into the Brunswick Street gutter. The wretched taste still burned at the back of his throat as he set off unsteadily across the road. A Black-and-White cab bleeped its horn and swerved to miss him as he stepped out from behind a parked Commodore. The driver yelled, 'You stupid bastard!' and disappeared into the night.

The drizzle gave way to light rain when Nick reached the corner of Harcourt Street. He pushed on past the Laundromat, where the redhead in leathers and stiletto boots, lolling under the awning with her hands on her hips, was a police officer breaching the *Trade Practices Act*—advertising a service she did not intend to deliver. The rain was falling heavily. The damp began to work its way through. Nick was wet to his thighs in his black stretch Levi's. Water seeped into his boots each time he wandered off the footpath and into the swelling gutter.

Nick turned the corner into Harcourt Street, intending to slip into the yard of the boarding house by vaulting the fence, just behind the old garden shed. He noticed Constable Redhead's back up team conversing earnestly with a man pushed, hands flat, head down, across the boot of the patrol car. The man's once-smart Italian suit was becoming increasingly dishevelled. Nick couldn't help smiling at the thought that the damp all-wool fabric would be steadily and irretrievably shrinking in the rain. He recognised the suit as belonging to the Legal Aid duty solicitor he'd been allocated last time he'd appeared in the Brisbane Magistrates Court on charges of possession of a smoking implement. *Legal Aid guy should've known the only good-looking girls soliciting on Brunswick Street are police out to trap a few players.*

Nick thought of Jade begging for him to draw her up another hit. *She'll be waiting.*

The police were enjoying themselves too much to notice Nick slip the bottle into his pack, then lift himself up on both hands to go over the paling fence. As he dropped through the vines to the other side, he took in the morning glory, the blooms ripe with that sweet rotten moonflower scent. He followed the path down past the empty carports, negotiated the bins full of uncollected garbage and avoided stumbling into the weedy beds. The path ended in front of the tool room, at the foot of the stairs that led to the back entrance to the room where Jade was kept.

Nick took the Stollie out of his pack again, unscrewed the lid. He took a deep swig. After replacing the cap, he kept a tight grip on the neck of the bottle with one hand and hung onto the rail with the other.

Up the stairs he went. He leant against the rail at the top and banged on the door with the old brass knocker. She didn't answer.

Nick descended the stairs and wandered around to the pale light of the window, struggling through knee-high weeds. He looked up at the dirty white lace curtains, hanging in the open casement, moving in the breeze. A glow that could have been a lantern torch threw shadows shifting in the blur of his lustful imagination. The shapes behind the curtains tossed and turned. Nick smelt the cocktail mix of male and female—of sweat, cheap wine and stale old cigarettes. When the breeze blew the curtains apart, it was barely possible to distinguish the interlocked forms. They clutched and sighed and groaned and whispered as they moved.

There was nothing to be gained by standing out in the back yard all night, soaking up the rain. Nick walked down the side of the house, through the weeds again, then sat for a while at the bottom of the front stairs. She'd have to be finished with Bui sometime. This was the only way out, now that the internal staircase had collapsed, leaving no safe passage down the corridor to the main entrance.

Nick took refuge in the tool room. The door to the little shed by the fence had been left half open, just across from the stairs. He pushed on it and entered. It swung back to where it had been stuck scraping on the concrete floor, leaving a gap just wide enough to let the light through to cast a shadow on the back wall. Against the wall, at floor level, stood a row of empty bottles. An old hessian bag lay in the back corner on the darker side, covered in a scatter of loose tobacco papers and discarded cigarette butts. Nick lay down on it, with his head towards the door, took the Stolichnaya bottle by the neck, unscrewed the cap and settled into spending a long uncomfortable night.

Nick's eyes became accustomed to the dark, enabling him to make out the details of the little workshop. He shivered as the warmth leaked from his bare chest. An old grey woollen blanket was draped over the lawn mower. He reached for it to cover himself, took off his backpack, pulled out the secateurs and gardening gloves and picked up the can of mower fuel. Nick poured four-stroke on to the secateurs, then rubbed the gloves all over them, polishing until they were so clean that anytime they caught a glint of light, they shone. He propped himself up on one elbow to get a better view of the tools that lined the wall above the bench. A baton-sized piece of timber was still clamped in the vice and the saw that had bitten into it lay out on the workbench with the dust and the shavings. The other tools hung neatly on the wall in custom-made brackets, an impressive array of instruments from which to choose.

Nick took a gulp from the bottle every now and then as he studied the tools. His gaze shifted excitedly from one to another, enjoying their destructive potential. He favoured a small hatchet hanging at about head height, just to the dark side of the shadow line cast by the door. As the night passed, he found himself continually returning to it. He became increasingly aroused, centering his fantasies on a visual image of the hatchet. He lost awareness of the room surrounding him as he stiffened, focused on the axe. The image blurred and jumped about, blurred and sharpened and blurred again. It seemed that it increased in size, feeding on the substance of his longing. The light reflected from the cutting edge glinted and flickered wildly as the axe continued to grow. It left its place on the wall and, when intensity was maximal, exploded in him with kaleidoscopic frenzy of colour and emotion. Nick came and lay empty in the empty room.

Just before dawn the room was at its coldest. The bleakness gave way slowly to invading warmth and light. The damp remained. Nick lay still on the hessian mat, covered by the grey blanket, his bottle half empty beside him. He was roused as the door above opened and the sound of pre-dawn goodbye shoes came falling on the steps. He raised himself on his elbow again and turned his head to catch a brief glimpse of Bui as he passed. His figure was short and stolid, with greasy black hair and dark eyes, the whites sticking out like almonds on a glazed Christmas cake. He was wearing Nick's old leather jacket over a khaki t-shirt. He looked ridiculous in cargo shorts.

As Bui walked slowly down the dim path, Nick struggled up onto his numb legs. The blood began to flow painfully as he shook the arm that he'd been lying on. Quietly, he reached up and removed the hatchet from its bracket, taking a tight grip on the handle. He blinked his way out of the tool room and ran with the hatchet raised above his head, catching Bui at the point where the path veered towards the front gate. Down came the axe on Bui's unprotected crown, cleaving the skull open. Hoa Bui fell on his face, his brains spilling out on the paving bricks.

Nick ran back to the gloom of the shed, placed the bloody hatchet next to his pack and returned to retrieve the body. He picked up Bui by the legs, gripping him around both ankles, just above his blue Converse shoes. Nick lifted one leg over each of his shoulders and towed the injured man, still breathing, bubbling and gurgling, twitching a little every now and then, back to the garden shed and inside the door. The transport technique could be likened to a man pulling a plough, with

Bui face down, so that the teeth of his lower jaw acted as the blade, breaking on pavers as Nick, like a Clydesdale, towed him, step by step, back to the shed.

Nick dropped Hoa Bui beside the pile of sacks that had recently served as a bed, then sunk the pointy toe of his long right shoe deep into Bui's rib cage, enjoying the feel of the yield, and the satisfying crack. Bui groaned and rolled over, conveniently giving Nick access to the front of the cargo shorts. Without removing the garden gloves, Nick reached down to retrieve the Smith and Wesson .45 that was tucked under the belt, down the front of Bui's pants. Nick tossed the gun into his backpack, then reached for the well-oiled secateurs. Bui continued gurgling as Nick slipped the secateurs under the front of the cargo shorts, near the zip, cut through the belt and went on through the fabric. Nick snipped the underpants, scooped a handful of Bui's shrivelled genitals and gave them a good hard squeeze before he began to cut. Bui gurgled, kicked and squealed as the tissue gave way and the blood began to spurt. When Nick had cut them clear, he took his prize and shoved the whole bundle down Bui's throat. Bui's arms waved wildly and his legs kicked for a while. He went blue. Then his arse relaxed, releasing a mighty stench, just before he came to be entirely still.

Nick picked up the hatchet in one hand and the bottle in the other. He stepped out into the pink dawn light and started up the steps. Jade would be waiting.

IT'S HAPPENING AGAIN

In the dream, Garrick found himself slowly walking up Brunswick Street towards New Farm. When he came to the Laundromat on the corner of Harcourt Street, a tall pale woman, with flaming red hair, stiletto boots and black leather hot pants, beckoned him from the doorway. In her left hand, she held a police cap with a black-and-white chequered band. She wore green gardening gloves, soaked with blood, not yet congealed, not yet maroon. In her right hand, she held a length of rope, the end knotted into a neat, tight noose. She offered saying: 'Your nurse has been with your patient. She is late for work at the hospital. Your assistant will also be absent. It's been happening. It's happening again. You will find her in the Harcourt house. She has worked late too often. The baby is coming, too late for the hospital. Do not call for assistance. When you find her, it will be too late. Take it, Dr Willis, a rope for your neck!' She moved towards him, gyrating her hips, swinging the noose like a lasso, puckering her lips.

Garrick screamed, and as he screamed, he woke, already jumping out of bed. Rachel tossed and stirred beside him. He remembered his grandmother telling him, 'Follow your dreams, Garrick, follow your dreams.'

Garrick pulled on a t-shirt and a pair of old shorts, slipped into his sandals. As he bent to kiss Rachel, tenderness and panic welled up all at once inside his chest, threatening to cut off his breath. Then he ran out of the apartment, caught the lift to the basement car park and drove recklessly toward Toohey Street. His tyres squealed as he came to an abrupt stop opposite Jade's cottage. He flung the door open, raced over the road and up the steps. The verandah was dark, even as the edge of the sun began to creep over the rail at its east end. There was no sound of movement inside, and no response to his furious knocking.

The speech of the redhead in the dream came back inside Garrick's head, somehow taking on the voice of Sergeant Moroney. He remembered 'the Harcourt house', then twigged to what Rachel had said Jade mentioned in her last confused call—the old boarding house, on the corner of Harcourt and Brunswick, opposite the Laundromat. He turned and ran down the stairs, over the road, and jumped back into the BMW. As he rounded the corner into Main and sped past the Night Owl, he thought he saw a pale woman in knee-high boots and a red tartan miniskirt, long black hair trailing down her back, jittering from leg to leg as she stood on the corner. He looked again. No one was there.

Garrick sped over the Story Bridge and into the Valley, squealing the tyres again on the right turn into Brunswick Street. At the Laundromat on the Harcourt Street corner, Garrick swung sharp left, and pulled up just beyond the spot where a tall redhead in black leathers leaned into the window of an Audi TT, stiletto boots cocking her arse into the street. The uniformed police were too preoccupied with roughing up the latest customer to notice Garrick's heart jumping up and down inside his chest as he exited the car.

Garrick ran around to the front of the house, pushed through the gate and kicked open the front door. He ran down the corridor, lit only by dawn sneaking through the tiny window at the end. His passage was blocked by fallen timber, crawling with white ants, the debris strewn about when the staircase collapsed. He scrambled over it, like an infantry recruit on a hazardous assault course. He fell on his face. A stench kicked up at him from the grey carpet, the smell of nameless dread.

Garrick pulled himself to his feet and went on until he came to the flaking timber door of room 6. Internally, the voice of Tammy Moroney said, 'This is the one!' From somewhere, as though at a great distance, he could hear his own scream as he ran the door with his shoulder, rebounded, then picked himself up and threw himself at the slab again and again, until the hinges gave. With another thrust, the screws wrenched free of their moorings, giving a scream of their own as they ripped their way free of the wood. As he fell inwards with the door, bouncing off it as it landed, thudding like a terrible drum, his nostrils were assaulted by the smell of acetone, almonds, excrement and blood.

On the far side of the bed, Nick Myshkin, shirtless and unshaven, lay with his back propped on the pillow against the wall. His right hand, still encased in a bloodied garden glove, held a gun. A litre bottle of vodka stood on the table beside the bed, more than half consumed.

The axe lay on the floor beside Nick, skewed to the right of the bed at a forty degree angle, the blade facing outwards, sullied by the soft white matter and other tissues, congealed and clotted.

What was left of Jade lay in the middle of the bed, wrapped in a torn black bathrobe that might've once been decorated with a dragon, her face cloven through the right cheek, her teeth in similar disarray to those Garrick had once seen in a tumour in the pathology museum. The gash extended through to the socket of her right eye, which protruded—terrible, vitreous, ruptured and dead. The robe hung open at the front, showing the wounds. The spikes of broken ribs protruded through her left breast, from which the blackened blood continued to extravasate and pool in the recess of her navel. Further down, it made a sticky mat. On the bedside table, under the old lamp, lay a methylated spirit burner, a tarnished spoon bent to a ninety-degree angle, a red tartan miniskirt, and a silky wig of long black hair.

As Garrick screamed, the delicate membranes that separated the compartments of his mind ruptured, and the fragments of his being ran together all at once. He threw himself at Nick.

Nick grabbed Garrick by the front of his shirt, thrust the barrel of the gun under his chin and fired.

The old feeling rose from somewhere round Nick's navel, travelled up his thorax to his neck, down his arms and up to the top of his head. A yellow light burst behind his right eye, and his visual fields suddenly narrowed. A freight train was pumping along in his head as the premonitory migraine burst around his eye sockets. Nick was felled by the flash that came before the lights went out. It had been two weeks since he had last taken Epilim.

BYE-BYE BROTHER

It must've been around 8.00 a.m. when Nick yawned, stretched and recoiled at the touch of something cold and hard. His head ached, assaulted by the light streaming in through the tattered curtains. Nick was about to reach again for the axe when he reminded himself that Jade was dead. He remembered that someone else had joined them. *That doctor, the fool who'd put the bitch on a porcelain pedestal. Like she was special. Princess Shit!* Nick remembered him from the hospital, acting concerned. *Kind eyes, wide, like an animal caught in the headlights. Idiot thought he'd marry her and somehow, everything would be all right.*

The cartilage of Nick's left knee clicked as he rose and reached for his bottle. After a long swig, he looked around and noticed the mess he'd made. Things didn't smell the best. The doctor lay still, but occasionally his chest heaved and blood bubbled around his mouth.

Nick dipped a gloved fingertip in a pool of Jade's blood that had not yet fully congealed. He wiped it across Garrick's forehead after mixing it with that pooled around the exit wound at the base of Garrick's skull.

Garrick did not recoil.

Nick, still wearing the garden gloves, picked up the gun from where it had fallen to the floor beside the bed, took Garrick's right hand, curled the doctor's fingers around the stock and laid it on his chest.

It was time for Nick to leave.

PART TWO
OTHER STORIES

RATSAK

When we returned from our holiday, we were challenged at the door by a twenty kilogram rat. Hissing gutturally. Gnoshing at us with her scissorsharps and flexing ratty biceps like a 50s comic photograph of the anatomy of Charles Atlas. I lunged at her with military precision. Would have gutted her if I had had a better bayonet than the financial pages of last Saturday's *Weekend Australian*.

'So you want to play tough, big boy?' she intoned like a dalek on a panty raid, lashing out with a vicious kungfu kick that put an end for weeks to my chances of a comfortable erection.

Alison, Tasmanian born, held tight our little Jonathon and sneezed allergic and defiant at the beldame rat. The droplets scattered like lead pellets flying indiscriminate from the snubnose of a sawn-off shotgun, each bearing human microbes. Doubly ratvirulent.

Atlas cringed when Alison sneezed again. As she paused to reload, the rat fled down the hallway.

We stepped across the threshold, finding that we'd repossessed a nest with carpet gnawed and jumping up to bite our ankles, so thick it was with rat fleas. The kitchen was a shitty mess with cupboards full of urinated chewed up cardboard boxes. Jonathon, whimpering, held tightly to his mum.

My tender vegetarian turned purple brilliant. 'Ratsak is the only way!' she said.

'No darling,' I responded more meateaterly, still clutching at my battered prairie oysters. Couldn't bear to think of causing any creature to drag itself around all day haemorrhaging internally. Could end up dying in the ceiling. Crawling round up there in search of rotting rat carcass with the stench no end of damage to the value of our real estate. And what if Jonathon should take the bait? No thank you. 'With a decent rat trap, we can kill them civilly.'

Harry at the hardware had no giant-sized rat traps. But he knocked one together for me quickly. Special order. At a discount. Pallbearer, I balanced it across my shoulder and carried it off home wrapped discreetly in brown paper. After Jonathon was lullabied and snuggled soundly in his bed, I dragged my prize into the kitchen. I baited it with half a kilogram of cheddar cheese and with a struggle, set the mechanism.

At around three, Alison and I woke to a snapping sound followed by a few seconds nasty scuffling and a series of high-pitched squeaks. When the silence came, we breathed relief. We settled back to sleep.

In the morning, when I went into the kitchen to unload the trap, I found my Jonathon with his head half severed, teeth embedded deep in rictus in my cheddar cheese. Ratvenemous in instant mortitude, I left Alison to phone the undertaker and stepped out resolutely to the hardware store. At the butcher's on the way, I stopped to buy a side of lamb. At home I cut it into pieces, painting each bait generously with Harrry's deadliest anticoagulant.

CHESED

It must've come while I was in the shower. I hadn't heard from Ray, although I'd been expecting a call for a week now. He'd not sounded well when we'd spoken a fortnight ago. I wasn't sure which I'd found more disconcerting: that he'd not been returning calls because he was struggling to shake the belief that I'd been fucking his wife Judy, although I hadn't been anywhere near Toowoomba since Christmas, or that the belief had come because a demon had gotten into him and taken over, a spirit of jealousy, unrest and false contention.

'*Spiritual Warfare,*' Ray had said. 'That's the name of the book. You must read it. I'll show you. Then you can buy it. And you must read it. And we must talk, before you come up in a fortnight.'

I could hear Judy in the background saying, 'No! Come now. Don't wait a fortnight. Come now!'

I tried to reassure myself that the sound I heard next was not the click of a rifle bolt being drawn back, but it was only that of the phone receiver falling onto its bracket as he ended the call.

I'd been very uneasy when I didn't hear from Ray by the next weekend. The following Friday came without him calling. I was heading up next day to stay overnight and show Leanne around the town where I'd grown up, and left, and why. I was very apprehensive. I called him and left a message on his voicemail to check if it was still all right to come around lunchtime on the way back to Brisbane. Then we headed off.

*

I showed Leanne the macadamia tree that still hangs over the fence, although they have knocked down the old house in Charles Street, and built a block of ugly brick flats where it once stood. I picked two Queensland nuts and gave her one, slipping the other into my pocket for the cemetery. When we visited my parents' grave, under the jacaranda tree, I left my nut there.

Dad's coffin had been lowered to *The Last Post* being played by a Vietnam veteran from the Totally and Permanently Incapacitated soldiers group, of which Dad had been a WWII veteran member. I remembered looking down into the hole and noticing a thin layer of green seeping into the clay from the grave next door about two metres down, but Dad was to lie a metre below that, waiting sixteen years for Mum to come and lie on top of him.

I remembered stepping up to the graveside after my mother's coffin had been lowered into the ground while a piper in a kilt played *Amazing Grace*. After the rest of the family had stepped up to pay their respects I came forward with my offering and plunked it down on top of her. Another Queensland nut bites the dust.

On the other side of the jacaranda we found the memorial for Ingrid Parsons, my American school friend Ethan's mother. When Ethan finished high school, he went back to the States for college. His parents followed soon after, but Ingrid was not happy to be displaced again. She sank into a deep depression and shot herself in the head, with a hand gun. In her suicide note, she said Toowoomba was the only place she had ever felt at home, so her ashes were to be brought there and interned in this cemetery. I'd thought she was such an old lady, but her plaque showed that she'd been only forty-six when she died, and so she must've been in her mid-thirties when I knew her, and only sixteen when Ethan was born.

We drove over to the older section, with standing gravestones, to visit my grandparents. Both my mother's parents had passed away in their mid-sixties. I remembered visiting Grandpa in his office at the back of the Ruthven Street shop where he had sold guns, saddles and second hand goods—a wheeler and dealer, with a used car yard as well and real estate and pawnbroker's licences. Things had not gone well for those who crossed him.

Then we found Ray's father's grave close to theirs. Donald had lasted only three days after contracting polio in the epidemic of 1953. Ray had been just eighteen months old. My mother was left alone to raise three little children for eight years until my father came along.

As I was reflecting on poor Donald's life cut short, and on the pain my mother had suffered, we chanced upon a grave in the old Jewish section. It was that young grocer Solomon, the man who'd donated the foundation stones for the Toowoomba synagogue, now St Stephen's Uniting Church, as well as those of the Brisbane and Melbourne synagogues. When the famine came in 1896, he bankrupted himself by being the only shopkeeper in town willing to feed anyone and everyone on credit. He died in the smallpox epidemic that came soon after. I had recently been reading of the concept of *chesed* in Jewish ethics: the attribute of grace, kindness and compassion, especially that arising out of the ten branches of the *sephiroth*, with its three columns of mercy on the right, three of severity on the left, and the four between them for mildness, carrying the potential for reconciliation. It seems that man Solomon showed mercy, gave freely of everything he had, then stripped bare, experienced the plague in its full severity. Such were the vicissitudes of a short but fruitful life.

*

Sunday morning came, and Ray finally called. When I got out of the shower and checked my phone, I found the missed call registered. We were a few minutes late, stumbling towards checkout from the Glenellen Bed and Breakfast, then out with the luggage into the car, so I waited until we'd left to call him back. I drove out onto Lindsay Street, turning to the left, along by Queens Park. It was a cold, dull, windy August morning. I pushed the phone button on the steering wheel and spoke to the automaton: 'Call Raymond Dark,' then tapped 'Raymond Dark mobile' when the two numbers came up on the screen. I was just about to turn right into Margaret Street when Ray answered.

'Yes, what is it?'

'Sorry I missed your call, Ray. I was in the shower. We've just checked out of the B'n'B and are heading your way.'

'Well, I wouldn't bother coming around here. Not after what you did last time.'

'What I did last time? What do you mean? What's wrong, Ray?'

'You know perfectly well what I mean!'

'No, Ray, I haven't been up since Boxing Day. I've no idea what you mean, and I'm worried about you. You're my brother.'

'Well you should've thought about that before you did what you did.'

'What did I do, Ray?'

'I dropped a bottle top. And there you were with Judy, fiddling with each other on the couch!'

'Ray! I love you, but you're ill, and you need to do something about it.'

'I'm done with you!' he said, then hung up.

*

I read that *chesed* as a character trait may not only result in outpourings of generosity, and of compassionate responses, but in enthusiastic largesse, in which an appropriate sense of boundaries may be lost. If a wave of *chesed* were to pass over a man, he might not only bankrupt himself in the interest of keeping his neighbours from starvation, on the basis of a commitment to the notion that what is mine is yours, with ensuing kindness. He might also behave as though he assumed that what is yours is mine. In a time when women were chattels, he might, caught up and carried by such a wave, have exploited his brother's generosity, and when invited into his brother's household, have considered himself licensed by that hospitality to make use of the opportunity to enjoy his brother's sisters, or his brother's wife.

I remember the nineteen seventies, when Ray, little more than a boy himself, strove to support his young family by working away from home on various infrastructure projects in the gulf country. These projects brought in the money, but ultimately did not contribute to the possibility of a sustainable marriage. He befriended a co-worker who was a Thursday Island prince, and they became blood brothers. Ray told me that one of the obligations of such a relationship was that he had to sleep with all of the prince's sisters. I gathered that he fulfilled that obligation enthusiastically, but when he caught the clap, that did not augur positively for harmonious relations on the weekends when he was able to fly home.

I also remember the nineteen eighties, when Ray believed that he could make it big in construction. He'd just made his first million dollars from his excavation business, and then gained the contract for the work on all the Quintex projects across the Lockyer Valley. Ray was elated—not bad for a fatherless boy raised in the dormitories of the Methodist hostel at Roma in western Queensland, while our mother had, in her widowhood, worked there as a cook. Then the entrepreneur Christopher Skase, the managing director, skipped to Spain with all the loot, leaving Ray unpaid and owing his subcontractors all he had. He paid them all, not holding back one cent for himself, and turned to start again, with all the ambition beaten out of him.

And then the nineteen nineties came. Ray married again and continued to strive to be a good father to his own children, and also a stepfather to Judy's. He worked long hours, rarely complaining of the pain from those old injuries. He even ventured out a little into property investment, becoming the landlord of a brick six pack, and of the shop next door, and the flat above it, in which lived a lonely guitar teacher, until the man fell foul of the rednecked poofter-bashers who frequented the local park beat in that city of gardens.

The millennium passed, and I found myself visiting Ray and his family on occasional trips to Toowoomba at Carnival of Flowers time, which coincided with the Leonard Cohen birthday celebrations at the Dancing Bear Café in Russell Street. I remember one of the folk musicians there playing and singing Cohen's *Anthem*: 'There's a crack in everything, that's how the light gets in.'

After the call, I was initially overwhelmed. I just managed to bring myself to concentrate sufficiently to safely park the car. Then I had to deal with the consequences of Leanne listening in and understandably assuming that Ray's macabre utterance was in some way connected with an actual event. It took some time to sort that complication and settle my own hurt sufficiently to think of Ray, and the possible risk to Judy. I made a rash decision to drive down and see him anyway, to see what could be done to help.

So it was that we were the first to arrive, after. If it wasn't for the caution with which I took the bends down the range road, and for the slow progress of the tankers and the coal trucks grinding down their gears as they blocked both lanes in the process of overtaking each other like gargantuan metal snails, I might have gotten there just a little earlier. I might have been able to intervene for the better, or else there might have been another chest penetrated by a bullet that day, before the final blast in the mouth that blew out my brother's brain.

A few days later, I was back in the old town again, helping with the funeral arrangements. I stayed at Vacy Hall, where a lovelorn teenage boy had done away with himself on the verandah, back in the nineteen thirties, well before my grandfather had come to be the one in town responsible for selling young men guns. The residence had later been divided into many rooms and set up as a boarding hostel for unmarried mothers waiting to give up their babies for adoption. The place had a reputation now, but I took my chances. My stay proceeded without any spectral manifestations.

At the graveside, though, as I stepped up to pay my last respects, a wave of hubris rose up, something that was almost the opposite of the compassion and wrenching sadness that I had expected to feel. Perhaps it was the old family madness threatening to rise and pass itself on. When would the epidemic strike? I wondered about that old macadamia tree, back at the place where our family home had once stood. When would the next nut crack and fall? I leaned into the hole and dropped a bottle top.

Just before I pissed my pants outside the toilets at *Karlsruhe Hauptbahnhof*, I was thinking of her. The train from Strasbourg had run fifteen minutes late. Time was tight for my connection. Then she came into my mind, and I found myself dragging my suitcase at high speed on its castors to the opposite end of the station from *Gleis 11*, the platform that I wanted. I clenched my pelvic floor and ran, with the toilet door in sight. Then I encountered a turnstile operated by a machine demanding .50 euro admission. I fumbled for change, panicked, and on came my latchkey incontinence. Then. There. At the head of the queue. In full view of the station janitor, whose face registered disgust. *Ein Vieh aus der Fremde.* Filthy foreign animal.

I found a fifty euro cent coin, slipped it into the slot and attempted to drag my suitcase through the turnstile after me. The bag stuck. I was through. I had it by the handle, but it remained outside, and I was inside. The kind man behind me, glancing away from the urine dripping out of my trouser leg and into my lime green socks, deposited his coin and squeezed himself in behind my bag as the turnstile rotated. At last my bag and I were both in the toilet.

I retreated into the cubicle, removed my shoes, my saturated socks, my trousers and my underpants, wrapped the wet stuff up into an Aldi bag and shoved it into a front compartment of my suitcase. I rummaged in my suitcase for clean clothes, hurriedly dressed, left the cubicle, renegotiated the turnstile and returned to the entry to the concourse between the platforms. The sign showed my connecting train leaving at 18:58, right then. I ran, pulling my bag behind me, reached the stairs at platform 11. When I was halfway up the stairs the sign indicating Heidelberg as the destination of the next departure switched off, leaving a blank screen. The platform was empty. I had missed my connection.

Then the encounter flooded my mind. On the first day of the conference, Karen McLeod asked me, 'Do you see much of Sarah Stinson these days?'

'I haven't spoken to her for about four years.'

Sarah chose that moment to appear in my peripheral vision. I turned to her, stretched out my hand and said, 'Hi Sarah. It's nice to see you again.'

She took it. Shook it politely, smiled. 'It's nice to see you, too, Ian. How are you these days?'

I smiled back and shrugged my shoulders. 'Well, I'm still alive, Sarah.

'Yes, you are, Ian! I'm off to the ladies now, before the session starts. We must catch up later.'

Yes, we had to catch up. With the same degree of imperative I felt about catching Ebola. I'd as soon catch up with Sarah Stinson as I would tango with a tarantula. The thought of it was enough to make me want to break out in buboes over my collar bones just so that I could ride the death cart as a means to a rapid exit. Just the thought of it was enough to make me puke and shit.

Fortunately, a benign old French colleague came up to me then and after stammering out *Je ne parles pas Anglais,* told me kindly that my French wasn't so bad but he found it difficult to follow my Australian accent when I was speaking in the groups.

To which I replied, *'Je ne parles pas Francais. Un petit peu. Je n'existe pas. Je suis rien!'* I don't speak French. A little bit. I don't exist. I am nothing!

The old man was good natured enough to laugh at that and overlook my provocation. But it was true enough. I'd sooner slip into a crack in a French culture in which I did not exist, rather than 'catch up' with Sarah Stinson again. That snake!

Throughout the remainder of the conference I found myself ruminating on the betrayal, on the way in which I had been made to feel special—that somehow, although she said we were not going to have an affair, we should hang out together, run some groups together, have coffee every Friday and have a platonic 'thing'. Sarah Stinson told me she had a crush on me, which provoked me to have a crush on her, and to trust her implicitly, while she pumped me for information. She was feeding Baron von Munchausen's version of my indiscretions into the gossip machine of our professional association, our personal circle and ultimately, the ear of my sulking wife. To Sarah, I was as special as a hospital for the deranged or a school for the mentally retarded— Special Hospital, Special Education Unit. Special Agent Sarah Stinson. I had become her special project, and she was on a special mission to ruin my life.

I avoided further contact with her. I hung out with the Germans and the French and avoided the Australian groups for all the social activities. So I managed to keep my guts inside my own abdomen and managed to have a good time by suppressing my conscious wish to disembowel Sarah. But when they served up *foie gras* at the closing banquet, I couldn't stop myself from imagining grinding up her sweetbreads with garlic and chives in a mortar with a pestle, enjoying them spread with a butterknife on mini crostini.

To the very end, I kept my resolve not to speak to her, and even though she was in my vicinity at the end of the closing ceremony, I turned my back on her, dragged my suitcase out the door and began to walk resolutely to the Metz Ville railway station. When I lost my way, and asked directions of a young Frenchman, he answered me in very fair English, offering to escort me to my destination. I had enjoyed my conference, had a nice lunch and was now directly experiencing the better side of human nature. I boarded my train after belting out the first few paragraphs of this short story.

We made good time to Strasbourg. I had no trouble making my connection to cross the German border and journey on to Karlruhe. Soon after the train pulled out of the station, I noted that we were running fifteen minutes late. I worried about missing my connection to Heidelberg. I was so weary after all the conference hype that in spite of my fears, I fell asleep. And dreamed.

I dreamed I was on a railway platform with Sarah Stinson. She was wearing a prim black business suit, with the skirt reaching to just above the knee, pantyhose and black stilettoes. She ran towards me, as best she could in those heels, her arms outstretched towards me, her cherry red lips pouting, ready for the clinch. I took her in my arms and kissed her passionately, lifted her off the ground and swung her round through three hundred and sixty degrees.

I woke with a jolt as the train pulled into platform 10 of *Kahlruhe Hauptbahnof.* I noticed that I had a boner. Must've been the French girl sitting opposite me. She was wearing a red tartan skirt, torn black stockings and Doc Marten boots. Quite enough to send the blood of a healthy Australian male of Scottish heritage coursing. I scrabbled for my bags and stepped off the train onto the platform, then down the stairs to the concourse.

It was then the confusion hit me. First the confusion, and then the panic. Thoughts of Sarah invaded my mind and, with them, the urge to piss myself. I think you know the rest.

Dejected, I dawdled down the stairs with my suitcase, travelled the concourse again, then rode the escalator up to the *Deutsche Bahnhof* office. I took my number and waited to be called. The clerk was sympathetic, and especially helpful, as I had bought a non-transferrable ticket. She gave me one for the next train, half an hour later, free of charge.

I made my way back to Platform 11, but it wasn't until I was safely seated on the train to Heidelberg, indeed, until it was pulling out of the station, that I looked back at the rails below Platform 9 and saw the broken body of a slight redhead in a black business suit, lying prostrate, limbs akimbo. I had dreamed of killing her with kindness.

JOURNEY TO GLASGOW

On the 09:46 to Glasgow out of Euston station, it was quiet enough for me to email my submission of a paper for next year's conference in Boulder, Colorado. Then I made my way through five carriages to the refreshment shop. 10:30, for me, was too early for a beer. But there they were in the cool drinks rack, next to the juice and well away from the diet Coke. I hesitated for a moment, then ordered a coffee and walked back. I reached into my pack, then settled into my seat and opened *Ulysses* to page 147, reading on from where Bloom was picking his teeth with his tongue when he comes across a vomiting terrier. He thought of ruminants before moving on to *Don Giovanni*.

Ulysses always presented a challenge to me, but I had made it seventy pages further than ever before, in the same flimsy-spined paperback Penguin edition I bought in my early twenties. It was not very long before I put it away, got out my phone and began surfing Facebook. I shared a couple of Star Trek memes, adding my own jokes as preface commentary. Then I find a post from my friend in New York, quoting Julia Kristeva on intertextuality. I shared it, with my added text: 'I think she is trying to say that if you've never watched an episode of *Batman*, you won't understand me when I shout: "Great Holy Rubber Underwear!"'

I returned to *Ulysses*, managing a few more pages, interrupted only by the conductor on his rounds apologising profusely for the failure of the air conditioning. The chances I might make it to where Joyce signed off 'Trieste-Zurich-Paris 1914-1921' on page 650, by the time the trains have taken me from London to Glasgow, Glasgow to Oban, Oban to Edinburgh and then Edinburgh Waverly to Oxford, via Newcastle, were increasing exponentially as the train moved on.

They took a nosedive when we came to Wigan, where a mob of rowdy twenty somethings got on and clogged the corridor, still drunk from their hens do the night before, stinking of vodka cruisers and complaining about the toilet, not confessing to each other which one had fouled it. They were a few minutes into singing raucous parodies of football songs when the train pulled into Preston, where they disembarked. When they were gone, the air smelled fresher. One of the quieter passengers yelled out, 'Just imagine being the poor bastards who've got to marry 'em!' The entire carriage clapped.

Then the announcement came: departure would be delayed while police searched the train for a missing prisoner. I reminded myself that I was on the way to Glasgow, where one of the bombers had been a junior doctor at the Royal Infirmary. I wondered about the man in lycra who had seemed anxious to push past the rowdy girls to get to the cycle racks at the far end of the carriage.

After a few minutes, another announcement came: that the train would be restricted to forty miles per hour on the rail to Carlisle, due to wet weather and potential flooding. If arrival in Glasgow was delayed more than fifteen minutes, we would all be entitled to compensation. Three casually dressed men and a woman in a business suit immediately jumped up, introduced themselves as litigation lawyers, and ran around the carriage handing out cards. I picked the one in the hand-knitted plaid jumper as the one most likely to be a terrorist.

I opened the book again, striving to follow the stream of Leopold Bloom's thoughts. Soon my concentration drifted to the koan my friend George had given me: *Lying down to sleep, let go of your body and let it fall.* My recurrent nightmare.

Then it got worse. A mob of women got on at Carlisle. If it wasn't for their lowland Scots, they could have been the mothers of the brides. They filled the seats around me and broke out beers and ciders from cooler bags, cackling loudly at every utterance of the fattest and most manic, all the way to Glasgow Central. I found myself recalling Bloom's sympathetic ruminations on the bovines entering the slaughterhouse. My sympathy ran out quickly.

I waited until the last of them had gone before retrieving my luggage and alighting from the train. I hailed a taxi and was happy to pay the driver the ten pounds minimum for the short trip to the Apex City of Glasgow Hotel.

When I got into my room, I switched on the flat screen and watched the news. The first story was about the man that the police sought on the train. He had been a terrorist who escaped from the kitchen of Wandsworth prison by strapping himself to the bottom of a catering truck. It was comforting to learn that he'd been apprehended, riding a bicycle along a canal in West London.

I pulled off my Doc Martens, opened my suitcase to retrieve my harmonica, pulled my travel guitar out of its case and began to play and sing the blues. I was halfway into the second verse of *CC Rider* when the guest in the next room banged loudly on the wall. I quietly put down my guitar and lifted my harmonica rack from my neck. I opened a drawstring sack and pulled out the pipes. I blew gently into the chanter until I'd filled the bellows, then let rip with the ACDC solo.

When I heard about one hundred and twenty-eight baby bobtail squid being sent to the International Space aboard Space X's Falcon 9 rocket, I was wildly excited. Here, they would be able to study the effect of zero gravity and the variance of other conditions that prevail upon the development of a life form, taken from Earth in its infancy, over it's lifespan. Under the microscope, they looked like translucent blobs with brown spots, two dark eyes and pseudopods that reminded me of catfish whiskers.

The first known infection was of an astronaut, an Australian medico who trained with NASA, On return home to Paramatta, Dr Julius Kovalenko, an intensive care specialist who worked at Westmead Hospital, experienced night sweats, griping abdominal pain, visions of strange molluscan couplings, distressing dreams of anal penetration by a spiked hectocotylus, which deposited a viscous fluid through the wall of his rectum into his peritoneal cavity. He lost consciousness, suffered a respiratory arrest, requiring intubation with positive inspiratory pressure ventilation. His abdomen distended and visibly undulated, over a twenty-four hour period, until his flailing form gave way. His bowels exploded, issuing forth a turgid mass of adolescent squid, shortly after which his blood pressure drastically fell. He was pale, exsanguinated, and promptly died.

The squid who'd left their host scampered across the gap that separated them from the medical and nursing staff involved in heroic attempts at resuscitation, shooting out hectocotuli into the exposed skin, the eyes, the nostrils, the mouths of the intensive care personnel, injecting sperm with what those few surviving witnesses described as an ecstatic humming of the last few bars of Fleetwood Mac's *Rhiannon*, then shrivelling and dying, leaving small pools of goo that proved highly flammable and smelt, according to one of the intensivists, himself a child refugee from Saigon, like the napalm ravaged aftermath of a tropical forest.

Fortunately, at the time, I had been five minutes away on the labour ward, on the other side of the hospital campus, repairing the episiotomy incision I had made to assist a baby's head to make it through his mother's stretched vulva without tearing her apart. When I heard the Code Black call, I had no choice but to take the poor woman down from the stirrups, hand her over to the midwife and run to the emergency department. I always tried to be the last to make it to the cardiac arrest calls. I did my best to avoid being obliged to intubate, ventilate and do chest compressions on dead people, especially children, after having to pass on the bad news to family members who'd heard the ribs crack from where they stood on the other side of the curtain. This time, though, I ran. Code Black meant one of ours was down.

When I saw Cindy writhing in agony on the emergency room floor, along with several other colleagues, my instinct was to rush in immediately to help her, but Dr Todd, the clinical director, pushed me back.

'Don't go anywhere near her without full PPE,' the old man ordered. That's Personal Protective Equipment: gloves and gown, overshoes, mask and face shield. Only too familiar, from the time of the Covid 19 pandemic. Several other doctors were already struggling to don the gear as quickly as they could, so I joined them.

Just as I was ready to go in, Cindy screamed and soiled herself explosively. That just ripped me. I saw the tentacled jelly thing burst through the back of her scrub trousers. I picked up a black stiletto pump that Cindy kicked off in the midst of her dying throes and ran at the thing, roaring. I wanted to bash the thing.

'Not so fast!' said old Todd, grabbing me in a choke hold from behind. 'Don't go anywhere near that thing without a flame thrower.'

So it went on through that night, we emergency physicians, battling the parasites with acetylene torches, sometimes setting fire to the curtains around the cubicles, then having to drop the weapons and reach for fire extinguishers. A number of patients managed to run out the door and onto the street after being inoculated by the squid hectoculi. It's too early to speculate as to why they didn't, like my dear Cindy, immediately succumb. They'd be the first of the ambulant host carriers. It's hard to know on whom to turn the torch, these days.

Well, hear I am again, fighting the good fight. Yet something deep inside me wrenches against the futility. I can almost hear my mother's shrill voice commanding me: 'Physician heal yourself!' My mother was one whose compassion organ must've shrivelled like an ephemeral flower for lack of watering when she was young, but somehow managed to grow an oasis of omnipotence, grandiosity and entitlement well enough in the midst of her childhood's emotional desert. I find myself feeling weak and frightened, wobbly at the knees and not at all confident. I wonder if this was something like my grandfather might have felt when he was hiding out from the Japanese when he went down with malaria on the Kokoda trail.

I was brought up as a Baptist boy, but I couldn't bring myself to pray to something that I didn't really believe in. If I was to pray, what would come out of my mouth would be something like Jesus' last cry from the cross, 'My God, my God, why hast thou forsaken me?' God forgive my blasphemy.

The only thing I know for sure now is that when I feel that griping just before my bowels explode, I'm done.

BARRY WHITE

Eleanor was despondent as we left the office of the behavioural neurologist. The doctor referred to me as 'a most unusual case of late onset Tourette's syndrome.' Given that it usually manifests in early childhood, it could be, in my case, 'a purely functional disorder.' He surmised we had problems in our marriage. The utterances might be my way of giving voice, involuntarily of course, to suppressed anger. Eleanor rolled her eyes when he suggested we consider seeing a marriage counsellor. I remained silent, hung my head. Then a guttural 'Barry White!' burst out of my throat. It seemed the doctor was not familiar with the mating call of bufo marinus. Nor was Eleanor particularly impressed. She shook her head and frowned at me. The neurologist opined that, if I was not prepared to take my own malady seriously, there was little he could do to help. I paused at the receptionist's desk to pay the account. I declined the offer of another appointment. Then we walked out.

It might have been the next morning, or was it the Thursday after, when Eleanor, reaching affectionately to stroke my back on waking, recoiled as her hand encountered a sticky mucoid substance that had, overnight, begun to exude from swollen glands just below my shoulder blades. 'Whatever you do,' I said, instinctively protective, 'do not lick your fingers!'

The changes progressed rapidly from there. I received strange looks when, in the midst of my working day, my thickening neck burst my shirt collar button. I stopped coming into the laboratory. Soon I was hopping around the house on all fours. This was too much for Eleanor. She expelled me to sleep on the front porch. I spent the night hovering around the fairy lights in the garden, jumping to gulp at the insects they drew. I devoured several small skinks. I sat plaintively on the steps with their entrails dripping out of the corner of my mouth and down my double chin, hoping that Eleanor would open up and be suitably impressed. I pined for her.

The epigenetic revolution that wreaked its anarchy upon my outward form made havoc also of my mind. My capacity for human speech was gone, but memories of wilful vengeance against the toad remained, nuanced with fresh loathing of my now much less than personal self. All those times I'd deliberately swerved a vehicle to flatten a specimen on the road came back to me, savage remorse blending into the nausea that accompanied the awakening of strange erotic imagery and compulsions to violent coupling with amphibians. I remembered experiencing something like this when Eleanor and I had a strange night after we each took a couple of puffs from a toad skin spliff that was being passed around at the Nimbin Roots Festival. I wondered was that where all this began?

My awareness of the cries of other males grew increasingly acute. I recognised some at lower pulse rates and more dominant frequencies than my own, despite the failure of my new form to shrink itself down to a normal cane toad size. I also noticed the response calls of several she-toads in close vicinity but found these to be of little interest. On the contrary, my preoccupation remained jealously territorially defensive. I decided to mount guard at the top of the steps, preventing access to any rival suitor that might emerge from his burrow with amorous intentions, hoping that his mellifluous vocalisations might steal Eleanor away from me, leaving me bereft.

So that was how I spent the night, too hypervigilant to dig myself a burrow of my own, with the intense humidity, the gingers rustling in the breeze, the scent of leaf rot rising from the fertile garden beds, the cane flower pollen drifting in from not-so-distant fields. Before the dawn came, I must've fallen asleep on the front doormat. I woke to the rumble of Eleanor's Jeep crunching on the gravel of the drive as she left for work. I let out one desperate cry, but to no avail, as her taillights disappeared beyond the front gate.

I noticed that the air was now free of the calls of other toads. A primal terror rose in me at the raucous cry of the sulphur crested cockatoos and the mocking kookaburra chorus. I hopped down the steps and took refuge in an upturned terra cotta urn. I trembled as a fat spotted python slithered past my lair. I slept as best I could, dreaming predatory amphibian dreams, praying for sweet Eleanor's return.

The last rays of the sun were dipping below the western garden wall when a little tremor in the ground woke me. Although I was not consciously aware of it at the time, there were now only three chambers of my heart left to leap. Eleanor was coming home. I poked my head out of the urn to watch the wheels glide past as the roller door rose and then fell after the Jeep disappeared into the garage. I hopped back up the steps onto the porch and sat myself firmly on the welcome mat. A strange vibration travelled through the floorboards on the other side of the door and out into the boards of the porch. It was no longer the footfall of a biped, but rather a thump, as though generated by a heavy creature hopping on all fours.

The vocal signalling of the other toads was just beginning. I summoned all the love I had and released it all in one low pitched bellow. I thrilled to the response that came from the other side of the door: 'Barry White!'

TAXIDERMIST

It had been a long drive from Manly, up the Pacific Highway, with an overnight stay on the Gold Coast, then the next in Rockhampton. I had taken a detour toward Emu Park that morning, to spend a couple of hours with a naturalist friend who invited me to stay for lunch. Like all Queenslanders, he was passionate about many things, not least his state's representative rugby league team. He was a lover also of the native fauna, especially various species of green frogs. He had just been honoured by the Wildlife Preservation Society for his discovery, and mapping of the habitat, of an entirely new species, which now bore his name. Like all true Queenslanders, he was also vehement in his hatred of the nemesis of native animals and domestic dogs foolish enough to take a bite: *bufo marinus*, the toad imported to Queensland from Hawaii to combat the cane beetle, in which it had taken no interest. The beast had spread its way west across Kakadu and as far south as the Northern Rivers district of New South Wales.

'Don't get me started!' he said. But I did. Just one mention of the toad, after a couple of beers, and he was away. It was rather late in the afternoon when I set out on the road to Mackay, my intended overnight destination.

I'd been warned about the notorious stretch of road between the village of Marlborough and the little country cane and beef town of Sarina, half an hour south of my destination. The Marlborough stretch was he loneliest of roads in the Southern Hemisphere, nothing but dry mulga plains, flat badlands stretching out to the horizon forever.

'Whatever you do, don't stop at night,' they said. Motorists reported strange sets of headlights coming towards them from the north, then vanishing just when you'd expect a large truck with a trailer load of southbound cattle to come roaring past. Instead, nothing. There were stories, some of them true, of serial killers who hang out along the verge, waiting to abduct travellers whose cars have done their rings and dropped a cylinder or two. There was a particularly horrible story of the murder of a married couple of skydivers, at two separate locations along that road, back in 1975. But they'd found those killers and they'd done their time. Or had they? Whatever the truth, the message to me was: 'Whatever you do, especially at night, do not stop on the Marlborough stretch.'

Just the same, it was well and truly dark around seven as I drove past a service station on my left, and then a sign on the right that pointed down a dirt road to the Ilbilbie Motel. I was tired. I'd almost hit a 'roo that hopped across the road in front of me at dusk, startled by my headlights. But I remembered: 'Whatever you do, don't stop.'

About ten minutes further on, I noticed bright lights up ahead, what I expected would be another tiny village. I slowed after the sign that said: 'Koumala Hotel 1 km.' I pulled up behind a RAM pickup truck and a string of variously modified dual cab Toyota Hiluxes. I stepped out of my Camry and inspected the site. The pub was an old wooden two storey building with wide verandas with wrought iron lattice work between the rails. I stopped to take picture of the tall, corrugated-iron rainwater tank on its wooden stand. It had been carefully painted to appear as a gold XXXX beer can. Then I spotted the large stuffed crocodile that had been mounted over the main entrance. Maybe this could be my kind of place.

I climbed three wooden steps and crossed the veranda to enter the public bar. The walls were decorated with the heads of large animals, most of them of the marine variety, apart from the water buffalo, the wild boar and the dingo. I was feeling confident as I took in the locals, who'd turned away from the flat screen to size up the stranger. It was State of Origin night. Queensland had just scored another try. All the punters at the bar were wearing the maroon jerseys of the home team as they watched the game going on in Brisbane at Suncorp Stadium. None of those jerseys was anything smaller than three plus supersize. There was substantial butt crack visible above the jeans of some of these burly farmers whose posteriors hung over the sides of their bar stools. All eyes were on me now, and the looks were hostile. I realised I was the best dressed man in town, in my dark blue blazer, chinos and loafers. I was in New South Wales colours and I wasn't in Sydney tonight.

I kept my courage and approached the bar. 'Would you have a room for the night?'

'I reckon we could,' croaked the proprietor, sounding sufficiently like a cane toad to be mistaken for one short of a mate on a night like tonight, with shoulders wide enough to have played on the front row for the local team in his younger days.

'But you're not from around here, are you?'

'No, I said, I'm from Manly.'

'Well you don't exactly look like the manly type,' he quipped.

The whole bar burst into derisive laughter. Then, a few moments later, I got the joke.

'I'm from Sydney,' I blurted out, more than a little nervous now.

The room booed and hissed. Someone yelled, 'He's a Cockroach!'

The barman asked, 'You're not a greenie, are you? Mike, show him what we do to greenies!'

Mike, one of the larger men, occupying the stool closest to me, turned and grinned, making a gesture to indicate a knife slitting left to right across an open throat.

'No,' I said. 'I'm a taxidermist.'

'What's a taxidermist do?' asked the proprietor.

'I mount animals.'

'He's all right, boys,' said the smiling barman. 'He's one of us!'

ABOUT THE AUTHOR

Andrew Leggett is an author and editor of fiction, poetry, interdisciplinary academic papers, reviews and songs. Andrew lives in Queensland, Australia, with his wife Linda. They collaborate musically to record as the Blood Moon Wailers. In addition to medical degrees and postgraduate qualifications in psychiatry and psychotherapy, he holds a research master's degree in Creative Writing from the University of Queensland and a PhD in Creative Writing from Griffith University. He is an Associate Professor with James Cook University College of Medicine and Dentistry. He was editor of the *Australasian Journal of Psychotherapy* from 2006-2011 and prose editor for *StylusLit* from 2017-2022.

Andrew's writing has been widely published internationally. His work has placed, been commended or shortlisted for numerous awards, including the Bridport International Poetry Prize, the Gwen Harwood

Poetry Prize, the Australian Catholic University Prize for Poetry, the Joanne Burns Microlit Award, The Arts Queensland Val Vallis Award, The Whitsunday Writers Festival Heart Awards Prize for Poetry, The South Coast Writers Centre Poetry Prize, The Arts Queensland Thomas Shapcott Award, The IP Picks National Poetry Manuscript Prize, the Tasmanian Poetry Cup, The Melbourne Poetry Cup and the Australian Songwriters Awards (Australia Section). His work featured substantially in *Verbal Medicine: Twenty-One Contemporary Clinician Poets* (ed. Tim Metcalf), which won the Australian Capital Territory Writing and Publishing Award for poetry in 2007. His first two collections of poetry *Old Time Religion and Other Poems* (1998) and *Dark Husk of Beauty* (2006) were published by Interactive Press. His third collection of poetry, *Losing Touch*, was published by Ginninderra Press in 2022. As a spoken word performer, Andrew has been runner up in the Tasmanian Poetry Cup, the Melbourne Poetry Cup and captained the Queensland team in the Poetry State of Origin at Brisbane Writers Festival.